WHERE LOVE
BEGINS

Also by Donna Fletcher Crow
in Large Print:

A Gentle Calling
Treasures of the Heart

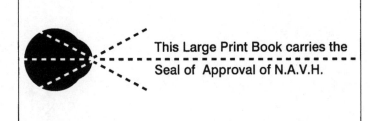

This Large Print Book carries the
Seal of Approval of N.A.V.H.

WHERE LOVE
BEGINS

Donna Fletcher Crow

Thorndike Press • Thorndike, Maine

Copyright © 1994 by Donna Fletcher Crow

Published in 1997 by arrangement with Crossway Books,
a division of Good News Publishers.

Thorndike Large Print ® Christian Fiction Series.

The tree indicium is a trademark of Thorndike Press.

The text of this Large Print edition is unabridged.
Other aspects of the book may vary from the original edition.

Set in 16 pt. Plantin by Minnie B. Raven.

Printed in the United States on permanent paper.

Library of Congress Cataloging in Publication Data

Crow, Donna Fletcher.
    Where love begins / Donna Fletcher Crow.
        p.   cm.
    Includes bibliographical references.
    ISBN 0-7862-1231-4 (lg. print : hc : alk. paper)
    1. Large type books.   2. Man–woman relationships —
England — Cambridge — Fiction. I. Title.
[PS3553.R5872W48   1998]
813'.54—dc21   97-30729

To
my husband, Stan,
who frees me to be creative

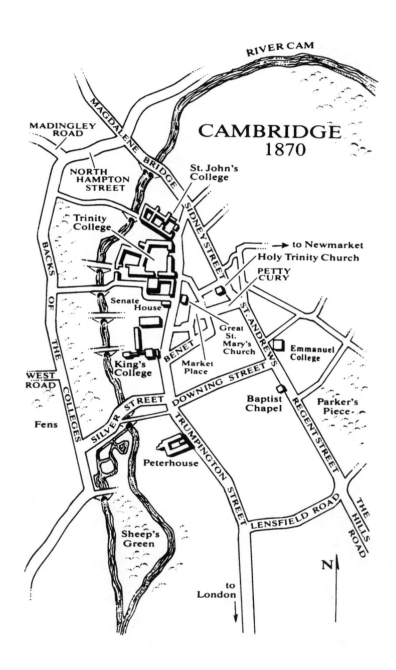

RIVER CAM

CAMBRIDGE
1870

MADINGLEY
ROAD

NORTH
HAMPTON
STREET

MAGDALENE BRIDGE

St. John's
College

SIDNEY STREET

Trinity
College

to Newmarket

Holy Trinity Church

PETTY
CURY

BACKS OF THE COLLEGES

Senate
House

ST. ANDREWS

Great
St.
Mary's
Church

Emmanuel
College

BENET

King's
College

Market
Place

WEST
ROAD

DOWNING STREET

Baptist
Chapel

Parker's
Piece

Fens

SILVER STREET

REGENT STREET

Peterhouse

TRUMPINGTON STREET

LENSFIELD ROAD

THE HILLS ROAD

Sheep's
Green

N

to
London

Miles 0 25 50 75

Kms 0 25 50 75

York •

ENGLAND

• Newcastlle-
under-Lyme

Sandon Hall •

• King's Cliffe

Cambridge •   • Norwich

Troy
House
Raglan •   • Badminton   LONDON

Bristol   Shoreham •

Bath   Tunbridge
Wells   Wells •   • Canterbury
• Brighton

LONDON
(TODAY)

St. John's Wood   EUSTON ROAD   The
Foundry

Regent's Park

MARYLEBONE   Tottenham
EDGWARE ROAD   Court
CATO   Chapel   ALDERSGATE

Mary-   Lincoln's   MOORGATE
lebone   Piccadilly   Inn
Church   Circus

Paddington   OXFORD   St. James   FLEET   St. Paul's
Cathedral
Bayswater   Mayfair

BAYSWATER ROAD   HYDE
Hyde
Park   PARK

Kensington   Grosvenor   KNIGHTSBRIDGE   PALL MALL
Gardens   Square   London
Ken-   Bridge
sington   KENSINGTON   Buckingham
Palace   Surrey
South   Lane
Kensington   Westminster   Chapel
to   Brompton   Abbey
Osterley   Parliament
Park   OLD BROMPTON   ROAD   Thames River

Chelsea

GROSVENOR ROAD

The Cambridge Chronicles

"There are so few people now who want to have any intimate spiritual association with the eighteenth and nineteenth centuries. . . .

"Who bothers at all now about the work and achievement of our grandfathers, and how much of what they knew have we already forgotten?"

— DIETRICH BONHOEFFER,
Letters and Papers from Prison

Preface

I conceived *Where Love Begins* after reading dozens of novels set in Regency England, all historically accurate, yet all failing in one vital aspect: These secular stories left the reader with the impression that English churches were boarded up at this time. Even funerals and weddings took place outside sacred surroundings. Since I knew that this was a period of great evangelical fervor — with Sunday schools, missionary societies, Bible societies, and numerous Christian charities flourishing — I sought to set the record straight.

In creating this historical account, I researched several figures of the time: The Countess of Huntingdon, the Duke of Gloucester, Robert Hall, and Charles Simeon. My accounts of them are true to the historical sources, often expressed in the words of their contemporaries. Charles Simeon's words are, as far as possible, his own. The description of Robert Hall, who could correctly be styled the Billy Graham of his day, is factual.

Many others also helped in recreating this vivid period of history, especially Marilyn

11

Taylor and a superb team of reference librarians at the Boise Public Library. I am grateful as well to Marilee Marshall for her patient advice, to Elaine Colvin for her motivation and encouragement, and to Hazel Flavell, who lived in Cambridge and served as research assistant and technical advisor. They helped supply the details of life as it was lived 160 years ago.

Women in the 1820s lived severely circumscribed lives. Few looked beyond their family and social circle for fulfillment. Even newspapers were read only by men. That Elinor's professor father provided his daughter with an education that went beyond needlework, sketching, music, and cooking was a rarity. Her society would have considered such useless, if not shocking, for females whose destiny was to attract a male and then run his household. Young, unmarried women lived at home and did not go out unattended or without a parent's permission. Such restrictions, however, were simply accepted as the natural order of things by upper-class women.

Men, on the other hand, had virtually no restraints put on their conduct by society — as long as they refrained from creating open scandal. This is perhaps why young women were so closely guarded.

A distinguishing characteristic of this period is the cant or popular slang used by the social elite and university students, most of which has passed out of usage or changed drastically in meaning since then. And unique to this story are the numerous classical references used by its scholarly hero. Although I hope the meaning of most will be clear in context, I have included a partial word list.

Another matter that often confuses is the ranking of peerage. In order, the six levels of hereditary title are duke (just below a prince), marquess, earl, viscount, baron, and baronet. Baronet is the only inherited form of knighthood. All except baronet are addressed with the title Lord before the last name, as Lord Calvert. A baronet is Sir with his first name, as Sir Brandley.

The Regency period is often called the last great age of elegance. It was also one of the great ages of the Evangelical Movement. It is my hope that this novel (although technically George IV rather than Regency) will bring that time alive in both aspects.

1

Sir Brandley Hilliard tore open the ivory vellum envelope bearing the seal of the Cambridge University Press. As he read, his chiseled features softened into a smile, erasing the deep lines etched around his mouth.

He pushed the assorted heavy volumes, pages of notes, and quills to the back of his desk and read the letter again, savoring each word. The Press "was most impressed" with the manuscript submitted by Sir Brandley. His correlative of mythology was "highly original while grounded on a solid base of scholarship." They would "like to see the completed work as soon as possible and would hope to begin publication within the twelve-month." Such news must be celebrated.

"Hollis!"

"Yes, sir." The servant provided by the college appeared with an equanimity that showed clearly he was accustomed to dealing with the whims of Cambridge scholars.

"Send to the stables to have Barrow saddle Emrys. And if Charles returns before I do, you may tell him I have gone for a ride."

Hollis laid out a pair of well-polished riding boots with white tops and a blue dou-ble-breasted coat with brass buttons for his young master before departing to find Bar-row.

Leaving the letter open on his desk, Brandley pushed his chair back, pulled himself to his feet, and crossed the room with a dragging limp. After changing clothes, he angled a tall, curly beaver hat over his dark locks.

"Come on, Page."

A brown and white spaniel scooted out from under his bed and trotted at his side out into the pale spring sunshine.

Brandley had risen at his customary early hour that morning when Hollis appeared with the ritual brass can of hot water. Com-pulsory eight o'clock chapel was, as always, physically chilling and mentally numbing. A chapter from Venn's *Whole Duty of Man*, monotoned by a bored curate, and two se-lections from the *Book of Common Prayer*, read at breakneck speed, freed Brandley for morning coffee. He took it in his room while doing preparatory reading for the morning's lecture on textual criticism.

His happy-go-lucky stairmate, Charlie, had elected to pull the covers over his head again and skip his class. He would later come under the harsh tongue of Mrs. Hazell, the bed-maker. How was she supposed to do her work when the bed was always occupied?

Now as Brandley rode Emrys down Trinity Street, he decided to stop at Thomas Deighton, Bookseller and Stationer. When he walked through the door, Mr. Deighton's wizened features brightened into one of his rare smiles that reached to the sharp, bright eyes above his spectacles. The glasses had so obstinately persisted in slipping forward on his nose that he had long ago given up the fight and left them there.

"That new translation of Ovid you ordered has come in, sir. I was going to send a boy around with a note this very afternoon."

"That's excellent —"

Two young ladies and their chaperone entered the shop to peruse Mr. Deighton's list of novels lately arrived from London. The young ladies giggled behind their gloved hands as they surveyed the titles.

"*Tales of Real Life,*" one read in an awed whisper, giving due emphasis to the third word.

"*Valentine's Eve,*" her companion breathed with a sigh.

"Oh," the first one cried, seizing another volume. *"Tales of the Heart."*

Then a new volume, *The Confessions of a Justified Sinner*, took their attention, and the sighs gave way to blushes and suppressed giggles.

It was clear, however, that their chaperone was having less success finding a title to suit her tastes. "My good man," she commanded.

Mr. Deighton looked helplessly from one customer to another. Brandley bowed to the woman, relinquishing Mr. Deighton's services.

"I'll be right back, Sir Brandley," Deighton murmured.

Ah, a titled gentleman was in the shop. One delicately gloved hand rapidly brought a fan into play to call attention to the dancing blue eyes peeking behind it. Beside her, a head of shining amber locks turned sideways to show off an enchanting profile and shy smile. Brandley turned his attention to choosing a new quill.

A sudden crash of falling books and cries of alarm made him turn back to the women. The chaperone's voluminous purple pelisse had caught on the edge of a small table stacked high with books, sending them tumbling in all directions. In the confusion Mr. Deighton's spectacles were dislodged from their precarious perch atop his nose. He dropped to his hands and knees to search blindly for them.

Brandley moved forward to help. At his first step, however, all thought of the disordered books fled from his mind at the look of disgust on the faces of the young ladies.

It had always been so. But no matter how repellent others found his disability, none loathed it so much as he. From his earliest memory he had shrunk from looking a new acquaintance in the eye for fear of seeing pity or revulsion there. As a youngster he had hated his inability to play games and his lack of stamina necessary to go to Eaton. Later he had resented not being able to serve under Wellington with his younger brother in the glorious Tenth Hussars. And he had loathed the unthinkingly tactless remarks of his brother's fellow officers who often accompanied Carleton home on leave.

As the women retreated in haste from the shop, Brandley tried to ignore their words — "odious presumption" and "unfit for proper society." He turned to help Mr. Deighton rescue the eyeglasses just before the man would have put his foot down on them.

"Sir, I must apologize." The bookseller gave his spectacles a push with a bony forefinger. "I am distressed that you should have

18

been insulted in my establishment."

"Think nothing of it, Deighton. Please."

"As you say. But please accept the Ovid with my compliments. And now, sir, may I serve you further?"

Brandley turned his attention to the matter at hand. "I'll have a box of your best quills, a bottle of ink, and a five-pound package of paper, if you please."

The bookseller took down the order — to be delivered to Sir Brandley's rooms at Trinity by Mr. Deighton's boy. Brandley thought of returning to his room to read the new book, but once more astride his mount, even *his* studious nature could not resist the feel of spring in the air. The fresh breeze, Emrys's tugging on the rein, and the bounding of his spaniel Page turned his mind to the fields beyond the town with their numerous bridle paths.

Youthful illness having placed most forms of sport beyond his reach, Brandley had become a bruising rider and a top-of-the-trees driver. Indeed, had he been so inclined, he could easily have won membership in the prestigious Four Horse Club.

But he had chosen academic achievement over trying to move among London's social elite. So he looked for recreation nearer to Cambridge. And few pleasures could surpass being out on Emrys with the spring land-scape flying by. It was good to feel his stal-lion beneath him while Page romped about and roused small birds into flight. Some-times Brandley tended to forget there even was a world outside the Great Court of Trin-ity College.

Sheep's Green Fen was dotted with clumps of yellow and purple crocuses and golden primroses. Newborn lambs tottered stiff-legged under the spring sky, and the sun shone in unclouded, gentle radiance. Some of the trees had already achieved full leaf, while others were still only lightly frosted with green.

Brandley gave Emrys his head, and they raced down the path. The light breeze in his face, the alternating patches of sun and shade flying past, the feel of his horse's hooves striking the ground gave expression to the exhilaration of his book's acceptance.

They galloped across the fen and turned into the wooded fields that would take them back along the river to Trinity. The winding path was bordered high on both sides by verdant hedgerows grown lush in the spring rains. Brandley was thinking of riding farther afield where he might find some jumps when his horse swept around a sharp curve in the road. Emrys swerved and reared, coming to a stop less than a foot from a small gray mare halted squarely in the middle of the path.

"What the deuce?" Brandley demanded abruptly.

"Oh!" The young lady mounted on the horse turned with a start. "Where did you come from?"

"I was riding down the lane, which should hardly require explanation. But whatever do you mean by blocking a public path?" His voice snapped, but the hand stroking his jittery mount was smooth and steady.

"Well, really." She smiled at her own mount standing calmly on a loose rein. "One might expect you to watch where you're going. As you pointed out, it is a public lane."

"Quite so." He relaxed into a lopsided grin that wrought a remarkable change in his stormy countenance. "But do you make a habit of blocking bridle paths? You might have been injured."

"Fortunately, there aren't many such neck-or-nothing riders about as you seem to be, sir."

"Nor many such obstructions as you present."

"I do believe this has brought us to *point non plus*," she laughed. "The only excuse I can offer is that I was admiring the view —

the yellow primroses in the grassy fen and the white towers of King's between the branches of those two trees. I was trying to memorize the spot to tell Mama about it. She's an artist, and this would be a perfect subject for a water color . . ." Her voice trailed off. She turned a delicate hue of pink and lowered her gaze, letting Brandley see that she realized how forward it must appear to him that she would talk with a stranger.

Brandley, however, had been studying her face for clues to more than her sense of social propriety. Then his memory clicked. "Daphne!"

She gave him a blank look and shook her head. "No. Elinor, I'm afraid."

"Oh! Yes, of course. How do you do? But forgive me. I felt I'd seen you before, and I suddenly realized that it was in a gallery in Pall Mall — *Apollo and Daphne* by Pollaiuolo. You look just like her."

Elinor's laughter was lively, all self-consciousness forgotten. "Oh, what a horrid thing to say. She'll do in the picture — except for the leafy arms. But only think what happened next in the story — bark growing all over her skin." She shuddered, then changed the subject. "Are you a student?"

His face grew animated. "For a few more weeks, yes. Graduate this June. Forgive me,

Brandley Hilliard, your servant." He raised his hat, revealing his dark wavy locks. He paused and gave a somewhat stiff smile as he realized how seldom he found opportunity to use that standard form of polite address. "Ah, Miss . . . Elinor I know, but since your groom hardly qualifies for making proper introductions, I must request you to finish it for me."

"Silbert. My father is Dr. Silbert, Master of Peterhouse."

"I am pleased to meet you, Miss Silbert. I beg you to pardon my interruption of your contemplation of the picturesque." He replaced his curly beaver.

She gave him her sunny smile again. "With the greatest pleasure, sir. But I must return home. My parents will worry if I'm not back before nuncheon."

"I should think so. Good day, Miss Silbert." He raised his hat again and rode away.

Once back in his room, he hardly gave Miss Silbert a thought until he picked up his new volume from the bookseller and came again on the legend of Apollo and Daphne. "In a moment her hair was changed to leaves; her arms became graceful branches." Brandley looked up from the page, in his mind seeing a charming young woman with her arms framed by the leaves of trees growing along the Cam. He wondered what Daphne/Elinor might be doing at that moment. . . .

Elinor, however, needed no prompting from Ovid to make her think of Brandley Hilliard. Even as she returned from her ride and Cobbett helped her dismount from Pallas, her mind was full of a pair of warm, brown eyes with curling lashes and a head of unruly, dark hair.

"Nuncheon will be served directly, miss." The maid's voice brought her from her reverie.

"Thank you, Katy. I won't be a minute." She flew to her room to remove her riding hat, tidy her curls, and wash her hands.

Elinor joined her parents at the Queen Anne table in the parlor. They could have been a subject for a family sketch by Rowlandson. Mrs. Silbert's Dresden complexion looked deceptively young. Only tiny crow's-feet at the corners of her eyes and graying streaks in the ash-blonde hair tucked under her lace cap revealed her age — just as a tiny spot of rose madder on her left hand gave a hint of her occupation.

Her husband's balding pate topped a round, thoughtful face that would have been somber except for the twinkle in his eyes when he looked fondly at his wife. They had married for love thirty-two years ago after waiting a number of years for Dr. Silbert to succeed to a college living. According to college rules, he could then marry. But Mrs. Silbert had been amply rewarded for her wait. Contrary to the predictions of many of her friends that she would find life with a scholar utterly boring, the Silberts had shared a quiet, comfortable life that suited them both perfectly.

Elinor accepted a piece of raised mutton pie from Katy. Before taking a bite, she demanded, "Mother, do I look like the Pollaiuolo Daphne?"

Mrs. Silbert, surprised by the question, turned to study her daughter's face carefully. A small smile of recognition suddenly lit her eyes. "Why, yes. Now that you mention it, you do — high forehead, delicate nose, arched eyebrows, and quite a rosebud mouth, my sweet. Yes, and the chin — such a tiny point to accent the smooth cheeks. But what brought this to your mind?"

Elinor took a serving of the aspic Katy was handing around, but left it abandoned on her plate beside the untouched mutton pie while she told of her meeting with the man on the spirited chestnut horse.

"My dear, you haven't touched your

food," Mrs. Silbert reminded her. "At least eat a bit of the fruit compote. What will Katy think?"

Elinor obediently took a bite of the stewed fruit.

"Did you say his name was Hilliard, my dear?" asked her father.

Elinor looked expectantly at his twinkling gray eyes. His unfashionable moustache curled when he smiled at her. "No, Princess, I haven't had him in a class. I believe he's Trinity. But his scholarship is well-known. A true student is quite a rarity."

Elinor smiled at this pleasant news as she sipped her tea. The soft, rhythmic swish of a scythe drew her attention past the French windows to the garden where Wattle was giving the grass its first spring cutting. She caught sight of the primroses beyond him and suddenly remembered the banks of the Cam.

"Oh, Mama, I forgot to tell you about the scenic place I found for you this morning. . . ."

The midmorning spring sunshine flooded the breakfast parlor at Okeford Hall as Lord and Lady Calvert sat over their coffee.

"Really, my dear," protested Lady Calvert, "Whipper is a charming dog — when

26

he is in the middle of an open field, but we cannot have him in the house. When he merely breathes, it puts out the fire. And when he wags his tail, the room looks as if Wellington's Light Bobs had marched through it."

"Very patriotic of him. It wouldn't do to have Napoleon's soldiers about." Lord Calvert took a drink from his steaming cup.

"Dear, only this morning Mrs. Wiggin came to me in high fidgets. It seems that Brandley's spaniel entered the kitchen in his usual quiet style, and the first thing Whipper did was to sweep Reeth's coffee cup off the table with his tail, sending the contents across the room. Whereupon Reeth chased him from the room just as Eliza was coming in with the eggs. With her usual self-possession, Eliza dropped the eggs as Whipper loped past her with Reeth in pursuit. Now really, Denton, have you ever heard of a greater want of decorum?"

"I wasn't aware that decorum was required of a groom," he teased. "Oh, I daresay you mean Whipper. My dear, it's only small dogs that must be careful of their dignity."

They were laughing together when the butler came in with the letter bag. "A letter from Sir Brandley, My Lady." He allowed

27

himself to show his pleasure as he handed the letter to Lady Calvert and *The Yorkshire Post* to the master. "If I may say so, I do hope we'll have him back with us this summer, ma'am."

"Yes, indeed, Wiggin. Things are never the same without him to keep us on our toes." Lady Calvert's fondness for her brother showed in her smile as Wiggin withdrew.

"Before you open it, we should lay wagers on whether King's Chapel has collapsed or the Cam run dry. Nothing less could induce my brother-in-law to take time from his studies for something so commonplace as letter-writing."

Gwyneth put a spoon of sugar in her coffee and turned to the letter. "Oh, Denton, his correlation of the Greek and Roman myths has been accepted by the University Press! Not that I ever doubted for a minute it would be, of course. . . . He wants to know if we plan to come down for commencement week. As if we'd miss it!" Her eyes still on the letter, she added a second spoonful of sugar to the coffee beside her.

"Will he be with us for the summer?" The viscount removed his quizzing glass and put down the *Post*.

"He says he hopes to have the first draft

of his manuscript completed before graduation so he'll be free to visit Okeford before setting up a residence."

"So your brother will be settling permanently in Cambridge with his research and writing. Seems a rum thing for a baronet to do, but there it is."

"Perhaps, but Brandley was never one to be dictated to by social custom." She broke off, obliviously taking another scoop from the sugar bowl.

"You are deep in thought."

"Oh." She started. Then she added yet more sugar to her coffee. "Denton, I suppose it's idiotic of me, but I do wish he'd marry. He said he never would, but still . . ."

Calvert laughed affectionately at his wife. "Who'd ever think you'd turn into an over-anxious matchmaker? When Carleton returned from the continent with Amelia, I thought you'd put your bow and arrow away. Hmmm," he mused, "but finding the right girl — now there's the rib."

"That's *rub*, love." She laughed, stirring her coffee. "But seriously, Denton, if he shuts himself up with just his books and his university work, he'll become a recluse like Papa by the time he's thirty-five."

"Without even memories to sustain him as your father had after your mother's death?

Brandley has far too much inwit for that."

"I hope so. But now that I know what bliss wedded life can be, I want to bestow it upon everybody."

At this, Calvert laughed fondly at his wife and shook his head. "On another subject, what would you think of going down early for a bit of the London season while I attend to some Parliamentary matters? Then we'll see Brandley at Cambridge."

"An idea of the first water, my love! I've some new gowns that have no place to go in Yorkshire. Shall we leave the children here with Nana or take them with us?"

"I'm sure you will know best about that, my dear. But I think they would enjoy the outing if the weather's fine."

"Yes, they would. Brandley does enjoy Peter, and Amy is turning into a little flirt to wrap her uncle around her thumb."

"Like mother, like daughter."

"Odious! I never flirted with you!" She lifted the coffee cup to her lips.

"That's certainly true. You made me into your friend. Much more dangerous by far."

"Denton, did you notice the coffee this morning? What could Mrs. Wiggin have done to it? It's delicious!"

Just then the door burst open, and their children were upon them. Lady Amy Elizabeth, her glossy black curls resembling her father's, toddled straight for her papa and encircled his neck with her chubby arms. Six-year-old Lord Peter halted his charge in the middle of the room. "Look what I can do!" A mischievous sparkle in his hazel eyes, he prepared to turn a handspring. Fortunately, Nana entered in time to prevent it.

"Let's all go for a stroll in the garden where you may turn as many handsprings as you wish," suggested his father.

2

The last of the crocuses were gone from the fen, and on the Backs the trees were now all in full leaf. But Brandley had allowed his studies to absorb him and had not followed his advice to himself to ride more frequently. He was seated in the Wren Library, but his mind was on the Parthian Plain with Troilus and Cressida. A smiling voice speaking his name brought him back to the present. He looked up slowly, blinking to clear the fog. His dark brows almost met over his intent eyes. Then he remembered. "Daphne!"

"I won't ask if I'm interrupting because I clearly am. I had to speak your name three times before you heard me. But after all, it is my turn to interrupt."

"By all means. Have you time to sit down?" He started to rise, but she waved him back down and deposited her heavy pile of books on the end of the table as she sat across from him.

"Just for a minute. Thank you."

"I've never seen a woman in the library before. I didn't think it was allowed."

"It isn't really, but the librarian is a friend of my father. He just looks the other way because he knows it is a great help to Papa when I can get the books he needs." To avoid disturbing the student working intently at the next table, she leaned forward. Brandley looked around, puzzled. He smelled syringa. In a library that never smelled of anything but dusty books and ink? Leaning toward Elinor from his side of the table, he discovered the source of the scent. He reached for the books on the top of her stack and inspected them — Aeschylus, Lucian, Sappho.

"Your father and I share some favorite authors."

"No, these are mostly Mama's."

"Your *mother* is a classical scholar too?" His brow furrowed in incredulity.

Elinor subdued her ready laugh, but she answered with amusement in her voice. "I told you, she's an artist. The myths provide wonderful subject matter. Her pictures are very popular in several of the small shops. Really, Mother's quite normal."

"And a classical scholar couldn't possibly be?" The twinkle in his eyes softened the lines in his face.

"Totally impossible — in a mother, I should think."

"Well, I wouldn't know. I never had one."

"Never had a mother? Oh, I should have

guessed — you sprang full-blown from your father's forehead."

His answer was a terse, "Hardly." Then he added, "But I must say, the idea of being Aphrodite's brother would be heartily endorsed by my brother-in-law. My sister is held to be quite a beauty and golden-haired like Aphrodite, now that I think of it. Gwyneth raised me, as I wasn't yet out of short coats when our mother died after my brother was born."

"You must have had a very uncomfortable childhood."

"Yes." The answer was surprisingly harsh. The memory of being passed from one surgeon to another, each devising a more excruciating treatment than the last, was indeed painful. Then he realized that wasn't her reference. His tone lightened. "Oh, not because of that." He shrugged. "One doesn't miss a person he never knew. Gwyneth and Carleton and I got on very well together. She was the proverbial mother and father to us even before our father died. But we were talking about your mother, not mine."

"Yes. Well, Mother's interest is certainly valuable to her when Papa goes off with the Duchess of Lancaster."

Brandley was thunderstruck. "Your papa does *what?*"

Elinor's eyes lightened. Again she muffled her laughter. "Oh, my yes. The Lady Blanche. Papa is a medievalist. He's doing a transliteration of Chaucer's *Book of the Duchess* into modern English with a brief history of the House of Lancaster."

"I daresay that's a relief!" Brandley said with mock gravity. "Mmmm, yes, I remember the beautiful lady:

For I dar swere, withoute doute
That as the somers sonne brght
Ys fairer, clere, and hath more lyght
Than any other planete in heaven
The moone, or the sterres seven
For all the world so hidde she
Surmounted him of all beaute."

"Yes, that's the very one!" Elinor made no attempt to hide how impressed she was.

"And what does the daughter in this remarkable household do besides fetching books for her erudite parents?"

"Must I confess that I also fetch books for myself? Bookishness is so shocking in a young woman. But I daresay I've little sense of propriety."

"Understandable with such parentage. Are there others in this extraordinary family? An older brother who studies ancient Chinese? A sister still in the nursery translating Mother Goose into Hindustani?"

"Alas, no. Just an older sister married to the rector of Chatteris."

"Oh, what a disappointment!"

"Yes, quite commonplace." Her eyes twinkled.

"And the daughter of the house — what are the books about that she fetches so clandestinely in order to preserve her reputation?"

"Sometimes I read myths with Mother, but I usually prefer Daddy's field of history." She extracted Walpole's *Historic Doubts on the Life and Reign of King Richard III* from the middle of her stack.

"Did you know there is substantial evidence that Richard did not murder his nephews? In fact, they may not have died at all."

He raised one dark eyebrow at her quizzically. "In that case, they must have attained quite an alarming age."

"Bacon-brain!" She smiled and shook her head at him. "Not until Henry VII got hold of them, that is."

"Who says so?" He frowned skeptically.

"Horace Walpole, for one." She held a book out to him. "But what are you working on?"

Before he could reply, they were interrupted.

"Thought we'd find you here, Hilliard," said the taller of the two young men approaching the table. He stifled a yawn and picked an imaginary piece of lint off his stylish morning coat. His tall, vigorous build, nonchalant manner, and rich purple robe trimmed with gold braid and tassels proclaimed him from the top of the social scale.

"Yes, but not with so fair a companion." His friend bowed to Elinor.

"My companions are always fair — just not visible," returned Brandley.

"Ah, yes, muses and goddesses."

"May I present Miss Elinor Silbert. My stairmate, Mr. Charles Verdun." Brandley introduced the casual one.

Verdun's black, rakishly short academic gown drooped haphazardly at the shoulders over wilting collar points, a neck cloth that had apparently been tied before he was fully awake that morning, and a coat most definitely not by Weston. But his charm lay in his open, cheerful countenance.

"And our friend, the Marquess of Widkham." Brandley turned to the taller man.

At this Elinor, who had been smilingly

acknowledging Mr. Verdun's second deep bow to her, turned brightly and gave her hand to Lord Widkham.

"Jack, I thought you were still at Ranswood Park paying court to your grandmother. How is she?"

"The charming old lady has made a miraculous recovery, my dear. I returned last Thursday, but I have been very occupied. My crammie hasn't let me out of his sight." He grimaced at his academic coach's tyranny.

"Yes, I should think not, with the term end so near." Elinor smiled as she removed her hand which Widkham still held. She turned to Brandley. "As you see, Lord Widkham and I are old friends. Our fathers were at Cambridge together donkeys' years ago. But I've stayed too long." She jumped to her feet, barely giving Widkham time to pull out her chair. But before she could gather her books, he had them in his arms.

"May I escort you home? Our studious friends will go on much better without us. Verdun's been assigned a Latin lamentation for absence from chapel. If he can just understand Hilliard's explanation, all will be well."

Brandley's eyes tensed as he watched them walk across the room, Elinor's hand resting lightly on Jack's arm. As they reached the top of the black marble stairway, they paused for a moment in a pool of light from the arched window above them, and Elinor turned a laughing face to Jack. It was some time before Brandley could wrench his thoughts away from the sight of the small, graceful Miss Silbert and her handsome, athletic companion.

"I say, Hilliard, about this lamentation . . ."

"What? Oh, sorry. Well, it's no more than you could expect with your Society for the Prevention of Cruelty to Undergraduates. Keeping account of fellows' attendance at chapel — and publishing the lists. Never heard of anything more cork-brained. Of course, you'd be assigned an elegy as soon as you missed once."

Brandley shook his head, but he helped Verdun complete the assignment. "And now remember to give a double knock on the vice provost's oak to signal that you're the bearer of a lamentation."

"Tell you what, Hilliard." Charlie held the Latin composition like a trophy. "I won't forget this. Do you a good turn someday. Count on it."

The gownsmen went their separate ways. Before returning to his room, Brandley stepped just outside the college gates to see what was offered that day by Crisp, the fruiterer. The man carried a large mahogany tray laden with desserts — lofty sponge cake surrounded by grapes, little dishes of cognac cherries, the earliest fruits of the season.

"Care for a few filberts, sir? Or perhaps you might fancy a nice ripe peach from the 'ot 'ouse?"

Brandley selected a dish of olives to sustain him through evening chapel.

A few days later as he sat in his room, Brandley closed his book and looked up. Charlie sauntered in with his Welsh corgis, Caesar and Chloe, at his heels.

"Ain't a holiday, is it? Only thirty or forty books on the floor. I say, what happened to the other sixty?"

Brandley scratched the corgis on their foxy little heads. "Returned 'em to the library before they moldered waiting for you to read them."

"What a hum! Scholarship can corrupt your mind. Just so I pass. That's all my honorable father requires to keep my allowance flowing."

Brandley laughed. He pulled himself out of his chair with well-developed arm and shoulder muscles and limped across the room to put on his smartly cut bottle-green jacket and check the folds in his immaculate neck cloth. Unlike those pinks of fashion in the ton, Sir Brandley considered it unthinkable to spend a morning tying and discarding stiffly starched cravats to achieve perfection. But since he did everything to precision, the sharp folds of his neck cloth were unfailingly accomplished on his first attempt and remained in place all day, never forcing him to take refuge in a loosely knotted belcher scarf as Charlie often did.

"Thought I'd ride into town." Brandley donned his fawn beaver hat. "Anything you want me to bring you?"

"No thanks. Just been there myself. Best to drive. Rain coming."

Brandley glanced out the window and decided his friend was right. If he got caught in a cold rain, he was sure to have a painful night of it. "Thanks. Think I will. Haven't been out in the phaeton for quite a while anyway. Come on, Page." The spaniel bounded after him.

Brandley had just finished his errands, which included a stop to see Mr. Deighton, and turned his team down Petty Cury Lane when the first clap of thunder rolled overhead. His horses shied, requiring him to exercise a light, firm hand on the rein. He was

41

only vaguely aware of a girl in a yellow dress on the walk just ahead of him. But when a small dog ran across her path, the girl jumped out of the animal's way and dropped one of the bundles she was carrying.

It was Elinor. Brandley reined in his horses and raised his hat in greeting as Page growled at the rolling thunder. Elinor came forward, smiling her pleasure at seeing him. Just then an even more ominous report boomed in the quickly darkening sky.

"What a delight to see you." Elinor brightened the dark day with her jonquil muslin dress and sunny smile framed by a straw poke bonnet. Brandley's reply was lost as another roar of thunder shook the sky. He had thought to offer to deliver her bundles for her, but this crash, closer than the others, changed his mind.

"May I venture to shock the proprieties and offer you a ride home? I'm afraid you'll get very wet if you attempt to walk it."

"Oh, yes, please." She thrust her bundles up to him. "Don't bother to hand me in." Grasping her long, full skirt in one hand, she placed her foot on the perch and sprang up lightly beside him.

"I'm afraid we'd both be afoot if I laid the reins down just now. This storm is making these horses dashed nervous. You aren't, I hope. Some women are so hen-hearted about thunderstorms."

Elinor's gaze swept the well-built phaeton, its black wood and leather kept shining by Brandley's groom. Her complaisant answer didn't evidence the least bit of hen-heartedness. "That's because some women don't properly understand a tempest. I wonder who Zeus is throwing thunderbolts at now."

Brandley smiled his appreciation. "But does your mother permit you to walk out alone?" He raised the ribbons and commanded his team to start forward.

"Well, Sir Brandley, I am one and twenty. Besides, there's only Katy, and I can't imagine taking her away from her tasks just to accompany me into the village."

Brandley laughed at her earnest self-defense. "Exactly what Gwyneth always said. How her solitary country walks did keep the tattletales busy! Once our neighbor, Lady Ashperton, bustled over to scotch Gwyneth's supposed attachment to the curate because Gwyneth had been walking alone to visit the vicar's sister." They laughed while on the floor at Brandley's feet Page continued his throaty growls at the lowering sky.

"How fortunate that we have no such

thing in Cambridge." Elinor's voice held a note of irony. "Excepting, of course, the time Mrs. Underhill drove all the way from Madingley in hysterics to tell my father that her daughters had been kidnapped because three ladies of the parish had seen them walking without their governess."

"Does that make sense?"

"As much sense as Mrs. Underhill ever makes, I fear." They laughed again.

Brandley had to turn his attention to managing his high-spirited horses. He had no time to contemplate the surprising revelation that this tiny, golden creature was one and twenty. Except for her intelligent eyes and poised self-possession, he would have been less surprised had she announced herself to be seventeen.

True to her words, Elinor sat calmly by Brandley's side, watching his skillful management of the team through the cramped streets of Cambridge. They passed into Pembroke Street and drove along as fast as Brandley could coax his jittery horses to go.

Just as he was preparing to turn his team onto Trumpington Street, a careening gig carrying two foppish dandies met them head-on. The frightened bay horse pulling the light gig was completely out of control. A thunderous clap broke over their heads and shook the ground around them at the very moment the two carriages passed on the narrow road. The bay bolted and shied, avoiding the other vehicle by inches. As the two bucks sped down the road, one turned back and waved his hat at the scene of their hairbreadth escape, obviously unaware of how close he had come to putting a period to his existence.

Brandley reined in his horses. "Of all the caper-witted, bacon-brained cawkers! They have no business driving even in good weather! Are you all right, Miss Silbert?"

Elinor had not made a sound, but had clung tightly to the side of the phaeton. Now, relaxing in relief, she grasped her companion's arm with both hands and sighed deeply. Finally, she relaxed her hold on the firmly muscled arm and pulled to her own side of the carriage.

"What a superb whip you are!" She managed a weak smile. "How you ever managed to keep us out of the ditch, much less avoid a crash into that witless pair, I'll never know! How fortunate that your skill with a team is equal to your skill with a textbook!"

Brandley spoke soothingly to his team and stroked the trembling dog at his feet before turning to Elinor. "Shall we continue? Do you feel collected?"

"Assuredly! If I hadn't been before, that test of your skill would certainly have put me at ease in your hands." The thunder rolled on and was joined by large drops of rain just as they pulled up in front of the red brick Queen Anne house to which Elinor directed him.

"Oh, the excitement completely put it out of my head." She turned to her companion as the phaeton came to a stop. "I've been telling Mama about my new friend, the classical scholar, and she said I should invite you to tea. I know your interpretations of some of the tales would be of great interest to her. We have adopted the new idea of drinking midafternoon tea. Would you care to join us tomorrow?"

Tea in the afternoon was something usually served only to invalids, but the novel practice didn't sound unpleasant. "Certainly. I'd be delighted, Miss Elinor."

"Elinor? What happened to Daphne? And now I can call you Apollo."

Brandley pulled back stiffly. "I'm afraid that's hardly apropos." He did not see himself in the role of the heroic sun god.

"Of course, I won't if you don't like it. But you've earned it, you know. Anyone with your skill could certainly drive the sun chariot across the sky."

Brandley relaxed into his warm smile, and he replied with a slight bow. "Apollo it is then. At your service, Miss Daphne."

Before she could say anything more, her father came down the stone path from the house carrying an umbrella. A stocky, pleasant man in his early sixties wearing country tweeds, he carried a clay pipe, and the aroma of tobacco rose from his jacket in the damp air.

"Oh, Papa, I want you to meet Sir Brandley Hilliard. My father, Professor Silbert. Brandley has been my knight errant, rescuing me from the storm."

"Very happy to meet you, sir. My daughter has told us about you. But, of course, your reputation as a scholar has preceded you."

"Thank you, sir. Your daughter has been so kind as to invite me to tea tomorrow."

"Excellent. We can talk more then. I'm getting a thorough drenching standing here."

"I'm sorry, Papa!" Elinor gave her father her hand and jumped down beside him. Brandley handed her bundles down to them and waved goodbye as they turned and hurried toward the house. But for once his thoughts didn't turn to scholarship. For perhaps the first time in his life, Brandley wasn't thinking at all. He was simply enjoying a warm, happy sensation without analyzing its source or meaning.

3

The storm passed as quickly as it had come, leaving behind a blue sky with puffy white clouds floating above a freshly washed Cambridge. The next day the birds cheered the return of the sun with their warbling, and Elinor found herself singing with them as she arranged a vase of daffodils for the tea table. She had added yellow ribbons to her soft green cambric dress and wore matching ribbons in her hair.

"You sound as enchanting as you look, Princess." Her father kissed her on the forehead.

"Oh, Papa, I didn't hear you come in." She gave him a welcoming hug and felt his rough tweed on her cheek, savoring his tobacco aroma. "How did your lecture go today?"

"The lecture was brilliant as always, my dear, and the students as dull as always, I must say. It's no wonder so many of my colleagues have turned their classes over to tutors. Is the world populated wholly with cawkers who come up to Cambridge for nothing but card parties and cricket?"

"Well, not *entirely*, Papa." She turned, smiling softly.

"Ah, young Hilliard, is it? Yes, I feature he is somewhat above the cut. Where is your mama?"

"In the parlor sketching. Will you take these to the tea table, please?" She handed him the vase of bright spring flowers. "I must go see if Katy has the cake cut properly."

Dr. Silbert received the flowers with the aplomb of a courtier, bowing over her hand. She giggled and curtsied. It had been her favorite game since she was a child, and he still called her Princess.

" 'I wandered lonely as a cloud, when all at once I saw a crowd, a host of golden daffodils,' " he quoted with eloquence as he carried the flowers from the room.

Just as she returned from the kitchen where the bread and jam and cakes had been arranged to her satisfaction, Elinor heard the knock she had been awaiting. "I'll get it, Katy!" she called lightly and flew down the hall. As she flung the door open, it would have been hard to say which was brighter, her radiant smile or the sunshine which flooded in upon her. "See, you are Apollo. Just look at the sunshine you brought in with you."

"Oh, no, Daphne." He clasped the hands she held out to him, completing the shining picture she made in the frame of the door-way with the shady hall behind her. "It was already here." And he smiled at her.

As she stepped back and held the door open, he removed his hat, and an unruly lock fell on his forehead. Then he limped forward into the hall.

"Oh, Sir Brandley!" She gave a small gasp, concern chasing the smile from her face. "You've hurt yourself!" Her hand flew to her mouth, and her eyes were wide as realization flooded her mind. The stiff coldness she felt from him quite chilled the sunshine of that beautiful day, but as he crossed the hallway in only two halting steps, she had no time to ask him to repeat the muttered reply she had been unable to catch.

That moment a streak of fawn hair raced across the planked floor and began to circle the pair with a clamor of barking and jump-ing.

"Mustard!" Elinor scooped her terrier into her arms, grateful for the interruption. *Say something,* she commanded herself, desperately hoping her voice would sound normal. "Musty, I want you to meet my friend, Sir Brandley, and I want you to be a good girl."

Brandley scratched the terrier behind her perky ears. "A Dandie Dinmont! I'm a *Guy Mannering* devotee myself." Looking Mustard squarely in the eyes and holding her chin in his hand, he quoted from the Scott novel which had given the breed its name. " 'You must remember that you come of proud stock that fears naething tha' ever cam' wi' a hairy skin on it.' " Mustard seemed pleased with this, for when Elinor returned her pet to the floor, instead of bounding off to her favorite sun-warmed spot on the window seat, Mustard chose to stay by the baronet, wagging her tail in circles and looking up at him brightly with her round, dark eyes.

"You have a conquest there," Elinor laughed, covering her consternation. She had felt that she knew him . . . and this was so unexpected, so . . .

Elinor stepped back as her parents entered. "Happy to see you again, Hilliard. May I present my wife." Brandley bowed over Mrs. Silbert's hand. Elinor relaxed the tiniest bit as her mother, sensing the tension in the air, graciously ushered their guest into the parlor. The room was bright with china and crewel embroidery and sunlight sparkling on the mullioned windows, but Elinor's mind remained dull with confusion.

As Mrs. Silbert poured out the tea, she covered for her daughter's unaccustomed silence. "I've been sketching a scene from the legend of Orpheus and Eurydice before doing an oil painting. I am most impressed by the Lorrain painting of the legend," she explained. "The figures take second place to the sweeping landscape, and yet the artist seems to have told the story so fully. I want to capture the joy of their wedding and yet leave the viewer with a sense of impending tragedy. Since I know you read the stories in their original language and I must rely on translations, I would be happy if you would look at my sketches and suggest details I may have overlooked."

"I'm hardly a competent art critic." Brandley set his cup aside. "But I'd be happy to look at your work."

Mrs. Silbert produced a large pad with pencil sketches covering the pages at odd angles. Brandley examined them closely, his brow furrowed in concentration. "These are excellent. Delightful. And you've shown authentic Greek dress and settings rather than draping contemporary Englishmen. Well done."

"Thank you. But surely you have some suggestions. Please don't hesitate."

Brandley considered the sketch of the marriage of the lovers. "You might want to include Hymenaeus' sputtering torch in your picture. It was considered an ill omen for the success of their marriage, you know."

"Yes, that's an excellent suggestion. I'm indebted to you." Mrs. Silbert refilled his tea cup and offered him more cakes. She ignored Elinor's untouched cup.

Professor Silbert picked up the conversation with an account of his plans to travel north with his family after commencement to visit the remains of Lancastrian castles as background for his work on the *Book of the Duchess*.

Brandley nodded. "Yes, that will take you through my native Yorkshire. You won't want to miss Knaresborough. The remains of John of Gaunt's castle there are well worth a visit. Richard II was imprisoned there in 1399, of course, and the fourteenth-century keep is well preserved."

As Brandley spoke, at the back of his mind was the dark cloud he had lived with all his life — he was a cripple. It had long been his practice to remain aloof from entangling social relationships. Though others might judge him cold or haughty, he simply accepted the restraint as his chosen lifestyle. Now he had broken his own rule, and this had been the result.

Cawker, he berated himself, *I should have foreseen this.* Yet he had no clear idea what he would have done differently. He had begun to enjoy her company so much too, and now it was over. The fact that Elinor had spoken hardly a word during the entire tea time increased his discomfort.

Elinor, likewise, was berating herself. *If I'd given it a moment's thought, I'd have seen that's not the limp of a simple turned ankle or wrenched knee.* She ached to reach out to him, to let him know it didn't make any difference. She knew he was on the rack, and she longed to make amends for her thoughtlessness, but she could think of no way to do it. So she sat mute. At least her parents didn't seem to be the slightest bit put off, although she was sure that her mother would wonder at her failure to have mentioned his limp — as much as she had talked of him lately. Her father probably already knew. Why hadn't he warned her? *But he probably thought I knew. Papa wouldn't think it very important anyway. It isn't.*

Dr. Silbert suddenly rose from his chair. "I must retire to my study now. Princess, why don't you take our guest for a stroll in the garden? I imagine your mother would like to return to her work too."

Brandley pulled himself from the chair and stood tall and straight in his coat of blue superfine and biscuit pantaloons. As the Silberts took their leave, Mrs. Silbert turned to give him her hand and her smile — so very much like her daughter's. "You will come again soon, won't you? Perhaps you would dine with us on Friday?"

Brandley bowed stiffly. "I greatly appreciate your kindness, but I'm not sure I will be at liberty."

"Well, soon then," she urged. She followed her husband out of the room.

Brandley and Elinor were alone in the parlor. After a tense moment Elinor came across the room to where he stood rooted.

"The garden is lovely." She held out a hand to slip into the arm which hadn't been offered to her.

"Are you quite sure you want to do that?" The bitterness of his voice was reflected in his eyes.

She stood looking at him blankly. "Pray, why should I not want to?"

"To stroll on the arm of a cripple hardly presents an afternoon of delights." His voice was harsh, the words coming from between clenched teeth.

She heard the pain in his voice, the bitterness that told her all too clearly how much he was suffering. She laid her outstretched hand gently on his arm. "Oh, Brandley, how *could* you?" Then the ache in her throat made it impossible to continue, and she stepped backward. This was going to be worse than she had thought. After a moment she managed to swallow the burning lump and regain some of her lively wit. "And to think I took you for a gentleman! That you could think such a thing of me."

"I only thought —"

"You only thought that I was such a ninny-hammer, such a peagoose that I wouldn't want to stroll in a garden on a lovely after-noon with a most intelligent and attractive companion. How anyone with so much book knowledge could be so totally lacking in common sense I'm sure I'll never under-stand!" When she looked up, she saw the doubt in his eyes give way to relief.

"In that case, perhaps I should inquire as to your willingness to stroll on the arm of a companion totally lacking in common sense." He held out his arm.

"That's much better! And you will please refrain from pitching me any more of that gammon!" She took his arm gracefully and bestowed her sunny smile on him as they went out into the garden, Mustard running happy circles around them.

She was deeply touched to see his vulner-ability, but she knew instinctively not to re-act in any way that could be mistaken for pity. After a moment she said thoughtfully, "Like Jacob."

"Jacob? Surely you don't suspect me of wrestling with angels?"

She knew the contempt in his voice was for himself, not for her. She returned softly, "Not really, but I do suspect you've been blessed even if you don't realize it. Has it been awfully painful?"

She felt him stiffen and sensed the conflict within him. "Oh, growing up was," he replied with a nod, the memory hardening the lines around his sensitive brown eyes. "A disease of the hip joint kept me on the sofa most of the time until I was thirteen. It has been arrested, but you can see the result."

Elinor smiled at him as she sat on a garden bench and patted the space beside her invitingly.

"I don't know which I loathed more," he said as he took the seat, "being pitied or being disdained."

"Pitied?" She looked at him wide-eyed, her astonishment genuine. "That's not possible. Pity is something one feels for an inferior — such as a wet kitten or a dog with a hurt paw. Definitely not apropos."

He was silent before her entirely original analysis.

"Pity is on a par with telling a girl over the age of ten that her dress is cute," she added with a wide grin.

He saw the analogy and laughed with her.

"Well, there now, if ever you suspect anyone of pity, you know how to handle her." She lifted her chin pertly.

"How's that?"

"Tell her her dress is cute."

"What if it's a male?"

She giggled. "Can you imagine telling a man he has a cute hair style?"

They laughed again, and the sun shone warmer.

Then Elinor became serious again. "Yorkshire sounds like a very lonely place to grow up." Her soft heart went out to her vision of a small, motherless child. She now understood the origin of the deep lines etched in the strong-boned face of the man that boy had become.

He shrugged. "Even London would be lonely if you lived on a sofa. I suppose it had its compensations though. I certainly would not have had the time to devote to my studies if I had been able to engage in the sporting life."

Elinor looked dreamily across the garden, thinking how this conversation echoed ideas from the *Essay on Man* she had studied long ago in the schoolroom. She quoted softly, more to herself than to Brandley:

"Presumptuous man! the reason
    wouldst thou find,
Why formed so weak, so little, and so
    blind?
First, if thou canst, the harder reason
    guess,
Why formed no weaker, blinder, and no
    less?"

The quotation from his favorite English poet brought a twinkle to Brandley's eyes. "Ah, Pope!" He picked up the lines:

"Then say not Man's imperfect, Heav'n
    in fault;
Say rather, Man's as perfect as he
    ought."

They were laughing together in this shared delight when Dr. Silbert joined them. Catching the drift, he continued:

"Go, wiser thou! and, in thy scale of
    sense,
Weigh thy opinion against Providence;
Call imperfection what thou fanciest
    such."

"Well done, sir." Brandley rose and then offered his hand to Elinor. "Was the 'Go, wiser thou' a dismissal?"

"On the contrary, I came to second my wife's invitation for dinner if you find yourself free. We dine at the unstylish hour of six o'clock."

Brandley looked at Elinor, one eyebrow raised. She nodded encouragingly. "Thank you, sir. It will be quite convenient."

The father was rewarded for his courtesy with an exceptionally brilliant smile from his daughter.

Later back in his room, Brandley realized with considerable surprise how much that conversation had meant to him. After he started, it had been so easy, so comfortable to talk to Elinor, as he had never talked to anyone before. He never wanted his lameness mentioned, but it didn't seem so abhorrent when Elinor approached it in her gentle, sunny way. She didn't seem to find him revolting at all.

But the afternoon brought its own problems. Difficulty concentrating on his studies was a new experience for Brandley. He was thoroughly disconcerted when, right in the middle of tracing an obscure Latin verb to its source, he found himself thinking about the Silberts. Not just Elinor, but her gracious mother and Dr. Silbert — so unlike his own father. He had hardly known his father although he was twelve when the baronet died and Brandley succeeded to the title. Baronet Hilliard had shut himself away when his wife died from a fever following Carleton's birth, essentially leaving the three children orphans years before his actual death.

The dullness of his Greek lecture the next morning did nothing to relieve Brandley's difficulty in concentrating. The gownsmen sat in a semicircle with copies of Aristophanes' *The Clouds* on their knees. The tutor distributed the parts. "Hilliard, please take the part of Strepsiades. Mr. Townshend, Socrates . . ." and around the circle until the parts were assigned and the translating followed, each scholar speaking his part in English from the Greek text.

" 'Come, would you like to learn celestial matters? How their truth stands?' " Mr. Townshend declaimed.

" 'Yes, if there's any truth,' " Brandley/Strepsiades replied.

The play ran for two pages before the tutor interrupted to read a short passage from a commentator, explaining the political aspects of the text. Then the interpreting continued.

As the reading droned on, many gownsmen allowed their heads, heavy from last night's wine party, to fall forward in a doze. At last the gods in cloud form took their revenge on the cynical teacher-deities, and Brandley/Strepsiades encouraged the deities, " 'Strike, smite, spare them not, for many reasons, but most because they have blasphemed the gods!' " Brandley closed his text.

"Well now, Hilliard, would you be so kind as to interpret the meaning of this reading for those of your fellow gownsmen who have deigned to remain awake?"

"Sir, the author seems to be decrying an educational system that was leaning to slick cynicism rather than to reform of morals."

"Ah, well put, Hilliard. How fortunate we are not to be faced with that problem today," the tutor remarked with a perfectly straight face. The gownsmen, roused from their repose, filed from the room.

Later, as Brandley sat in his final English lecture, his mind went back to Aristophanes' lines. He had never been called on, as Strepsiades had, to consider his belief in a deity. Zeus certainly commanded attention as a literary figure, but was he drawn on reality? Did the God the chaplain read of every morning and evening in chapel have any more substance than the clouds Socrates believed in? And if there was such a deity, did He then control the lives and destinies of mortals?

It was a question that had held no interest for him before, but he realized that if he were to view the universe and all in it as ordered of God, he would have to submit to this God. How much easier it would have been to do that before he met Elinor.

"Hilliard —" The vice-provost's voice penetrated Brandley's thoughts, and the scholar realized that the lecturer had halted midsentence in his reading of Locke and was waiting for Brandley to fill in the breach.

Brandley took a breath and seized at the main idea running through Locke's essay. "Sensation and reflection, sir," he replied.

The answer was inexact, but it served.

Upon leaving class, he felt a strong desire to share his new thoughts with another. Stopping in his room only long enough to remove his cap and gown and to put on his top hat, he made his way to the stables for Emrys.

Evening shadows were lengthening before Brandley rode slowly back to college. Indeed, had not chapel attendance been strictly enforced, he would have stayed longer in Elinor's company. As he rode, however, it wasn't the intellectual content of their discussion that occupied his mind, but rather the strong desire he felt for her company, the warmth he felt at her smile, the pleasure he experienced in making her happy. Such sensations, such friendship were new to him and rather alarming but not something to be avoided. Indeed, in the following days Sir Brandley became a frequent caller at the Silbert residence.

4

And then it was time for Brandley to take his degree exams. He spent four days seated on the three-legged stool from which the Cambridge tripos exam took its name, disputing with an examiner on Latin essays dealing with mathematics and philosophy. The first two days covered mathematics; the third day dealt with Locke's *Essay on the Human Understanding* and Paley's *Moral Philosophy and Evidences of Christianity*. On the fourth day he translated passages from the first six books of the *Iliad* and the *Aeneid*. Every interrogation called into focus all of his personal scholarship and challenged the academics of Trinity College where the classics were far better taught than in any other college in the university. Each day he left the Senate House with an aching head, cotton-wool mouth, and exhausted body. Yet he felt pleasantly exhilarated and stimulated. He hoped to achieve a double first class and earn the honor of senior wrangler position at graduation.

He had been equally impervious to the pale sunshine that shone in the high windows of the examination room early in the week and to the rain that dripped against them on the third day. But on the fourth day, when he emerged lighthearted and victorious, not to say a bit lightheaded, he drew deep breaths of the reviving fresh air and recalled his engagement to dine with the Silberts that evening.

There was scarcely time to change, but he showed no sign of rush when he arrived at his hosts' home. His broad shoulders and trim build were shown off to perfection by the close-fitting black evening clothes, French silk waistcoat, snowy white shirt and neck cloth tied in the precise mathematical style.

Katy had outdone herself on the dinner. It was her first time to serve a nobleman. There was no use telling her a baronet ranked at the bottom of the nobility scale. She couldn't have been more elated had all the dukes in the kingdom been coming to sample her cooking. Mrs. Silbert was sure that two soups were quite enough, but Katy protested, "We can't have the young lord thinking we keep a poor table, I'm sure." In the end it was simpler to let Katy have her way. The three soups preceded a roast sirloin, a fricassee of chicken, a broiled stuffed haddock, side dishes of light suet dumplings, carrots, turnips, and potatoes.

Brandley ate with relish and lavished praise on the cook, which sent Katy scurrying back to the kitchen delighted, her color as bright as her shining eyes. Even more than the food, however, the novelty of being part of a family group gathered around a dinner table appealed to him. They treated him like a member of the family, including him in their openness and warmth. He admired the charm of the candle-lit table with the centerpiece of garden flowers Elinor had arranged. But what impressed him most was the family's undisguised, unselfconscious affection for each other. Not that his own mealtimes with Gwyneth had been cold or stilted — and when she married Calvert and Brandley had made his home with them, their dinner conversations were full of cheerful, casual banter. What was it that attracted him so tonight? He looked from face to face, trying to isolate the difference. Then Elinor's father called her "Princess" in his fond way, and Brandley saw the answer in the professor's eyes.

His thoughts returned to the conversation as Dr. Silbert outlined his summer travel plans to Lancastrian castles. "Have you decided to visit Knaresborough, sir?"

"Yes, yes, certainly. Your recommendation was just enough to tip the scale in its favor."

"Then you must break your journey at Harrogate. My brother-in-law's home, Okeford Hall, is quite near there. It's beautiful country." Okeford was Lord Calvert's ancestral home, seat of the Viscounts Calvert through six generations. Since Gwyneth became Lady Calvert, it had been Brandley's home too. "If you hunt or fish, the area provides excellent sport," Brandley concluded.

"Yes, indeed I do. I fancy myself quite handy with a rod. And if the fish aren't biting, it's an excellent opportunity for solitude with a book."

Brandley laughed in agreement. "Quite my opinion too. I admit I have often found myself wishing the silly things would quit biting so I'd have an excuse to put my rod down."

"Will you be there this summer, Brandley?" asked Elinor.

Brandley's straightforward answer put to rest any fears she might have had of sounding overly bold. "Yes, I daresay I will. I plan to go north with Gwyneth and Denton right after graduation and return in late August to continue my research. I must admit I dread the thought of the scramble of hunting for a house, interviewing housekeepers, and goodness knows what all else."

"Brandley, I'm afraid your mind must not run to the practical." Elinor shook her head.

Mrs. Silbert rose and suggested they retire to the library until the tea came in. Although the day was warm, the evening air had turned rather sharp, threatening rain, so a crackling fire was burning on the grate. Mustard dozed on the hearth, but when Brandley entered, she ran to his side, waggling her whole body in greeting. She was rewarded with a bit of biscuit her new friend had tucked into his pocket for her.

Professor Silbert brought out his chessboard. Elinor declined to play, saying she would rather watch her father and Brandley. She seated herself on a stool between them while Mustard made herself cozy at Brandley's feet. Mrs. Silbert chose to sit quietly by the window with her embroidery, a branched candlestick lighting her intricate work.

As Brandley waited for the professor to counter a particularly skillful move, he looked around the library where the flickering flames danced on the old leather book covers with their gold embossing and turned the fine-grained wood paneling into moire. The contentment in the room was palpable.

It was a new experience for Brandley to be more aware of the atmosphere of the room than of the magnetic attraction of the books. His eyes caught Elinor's, and they exchanged smiles as he watched the firelight make highlights on her hair and felt the joy of her presence. But then Dr. Silbert made up his mind to castle, and Brandley's mind returned to the game.

A few moves later, Silbert exclaimed a jubilant and hard won "Checkmate!"

Just then Katy entered the room. "Lord Widkham," she announced. The spell was broken as Jack's presence filled the room. He bowed elegantly to his hostess and took Dr. Silbert's hand affably. The Silberts were all most courteous in their welcomes, but Brandley couldn't help feeling that Elinor was more cordial than mere propriety demanded. Jack's manner certainly left no doubt about which member of the family he had come to visit as he took Elinor's hand and kissed it lightly with a bow.

Jackanapes! Brandley thought darkly. He had always been more at ease with books than with people, which had led many to see him as self-centered. But books were safer than people. He would never feel this stab of pain if a tonish young lord snatched a favorite book from him. His sense of the ridiculous came to his rescue with that image, and he smiled as Katy entered again, this time with a tea tray.

"I've come to invite you to an alfresco party we're getting up for next Saturday," Jack said as he sipped his tea. "The strawberries will be in peak then, and we'll have a berrying party at Ranswood Park. We are rather famous for our early berries, you know."

Elinor clasped her hands and beamed. "Oh, Jack, what fun! I *am* fond of strawberries! Who will be in the party?"

"A modest group, my dear. Verdun, the Misses Underhill. Mrs. Underhill will be sending their governess. And you, Miss Elinor. And Hilliard." If Sir Brandley's inclusion was an afterthought, the glib Lord Widkham gave no sign. Elinor's delight in the plan made Brandley reluctant to refuse.

"Why certainly," said Mrs. Silbert. "If Miss Rashton is to attend the Underhill girls, her chaperonage should be adequate. Will you ride or drive?"

"Oh, let's ride. I'd far rather on a fine day — it simply must be a fine day! Brandley, why don't you and Charlie ride over here, and we can go together to the Underhills?"

Much as he would have liked to decline, Brandley could see no way out that wouldn't appear boorish. So it was settled.

As Brandley's first draft of his manuscript was due at the press the following week, he had little time for anything but rewriting, clarifying, and polishing the opus that would launch his career. His desire to call at the Silberts had to be suppressed since the temptation appeared to him with alarming frequency.

Elinor, however, had no such consuming demands. Her week dragged by on very slow feet. Once her pale blue riding habit with the trim jacket and ruffled blouse was brushed and pressed and the matching hat with curling feather tried on numerous times to assure her that it was becoming, she could find nothing else to do to ready herself for the party. She turned naturally to her reading. Remembering the fun she and Brandley had had quoting Pope, she decided to reread the *Essay on Man.*

5

Saturday dawned golden and cloudless, putting to rest all fears of a cold drizzle spoiling the day. Brandley and Charlie met Elinor at her home to escort her to the Underhills. As they set off in high spirits at ten o'clock, they were waved away by her father. A frustrated Mustard was much incensed at not being allowed to come.

They rode through the parkland along the banks of the Cam where water beetles danced in the sun on the river's surface. Waterfowl drifted in the placid water until a barge laden with coal for the Cambridge market approached, and they scattered before the barge horse walking chest-deep in the water, raising whorls of mud as it made its way upstream.

Looking across the river through the trees to the Backs, Elinor took in the grace of the willows trailing their supple branches in the green depths and the symmetry of the series of bridges from the gardens of the various colleges. "I do think Capability Brown improved the perspective vastly when he flattened King's garden and decreed that cows should be kept grazing on the Back." Elinor stopped Pallas and smiled at the scene before her.

"It does give it a distinctively rural air," Brandley agreed. Then he added with a mischievous grin, "Another pause for contemplation of the picturesque, Miss Silbert?"

Elinor's face lighted with memory. "I daresay, Sir Brandley. But at least this time there doesn't seem to be a break-neck horseman bearing down on me."

"Quite right. Much safer to keep such care-for-nothings under surveillance."

"I see you've guessed my strategy."

"I say, are you two going to nitter-natter all day, or are we going to Madingley?" Charlie interrupted.

They proceeded up Queen's Road past Clare College, Trinity, and St. John's. Brandley's attention, however, was not on the fine buildings in the distance, but on the young woman a few paces ahead of him and on his own emotions, which he usually ignored. Not since his early youth had he cared so for the opinion of another or so loathed his infirmity. With part of himself he welcomed the growing friendship; but with another he resisted it. He could not help but wonder if the gods were using him for their sport, leading him deeper into a relationship that could only end in heart-break.

Suddenly a lively party in a punt glided into view. Girls with ruffled parasols were laughing at a joke that had apparently come from the young man sitting fore in the flat narrow boat. Another young man, standing aft, propelled their long skiff with a lengthy pole. He was doing well until a crew in a six-oar canoe overtook them, and the punter misjudged the distance needed for passing. The scrunch of wood on wood and the startled voices of the boaters reached the riders who halted to watch. Elinor held her breath until the shallow boats settled themselves, and the revelers continued on their way.

"Rum thing to do, punting." Charlie shook his head. "Got to have more hair than wit to enjoy it."

"Apparently you've had experience, Charlie." Brandley watched the punter raise his arms above the pole and turn to thrust it backward. The punt shot under St. John's bridge as the riders once more urged their horses forward.

"Well, I have. Learned right off too. Pole pours water up your sleeve. Worse, if you hold on to it when you push, you'll be left clinging to it like a monkey on a stick while the punt slides away. Fellow'd have to be a dashed noddicock to enjoy it."

Elinor broke into peals of laughter at this picture. "Charlie, don't tell me that actually happened to you!"

"Close enough to put me off the pastime."

The path wound northeastward away from the river where a flock of sheep grazed in the lush grass.

"Look what meticulous gardeners the sheep are." Elinor gestured toward a pasture dotted with dark green oaks. "The bottoms of the oak trees are all pruned exactly even."

Leaving the oaks, they rode through well-kept fields of wheat, potatoes, and flax surrounded by hedgerows, finally arriving at Madingley. Miss Faith Underhill had to return to the vicarage only once to pick up a forgotten article; and the group had not even passed out of the lane yet before her sister Hope remembered her parasol left on the bench by the breakfast table.

"Is there a third Miss Underhill?" Brandley asked Elinor while they awaited Hope's return.

"Surely, sir, you aren't suggesting that the estimable vicar might be possessed of Faith and Hope, but no Charity?"

"Pity there wasn't a fourth; I do wonder what they would have named her."

"Did you notice that the ladies of the vicarage are proclaiming their literacy in their dress?" Elinor asked.

"No. Whatever do you mean?"

"I would hardly have suspected you to be an avid reader of novels, but one of Miss Austen's books includes a strawberrying party, and what do you suppose the parson's wife wore?"

Brandley surveyed Faith Underhill. "Could it possibly have been a broad-brimmed hat, a dress with a flounce, and a basket tied on her arm?"

"Oh, my yes. How did you ever guess? Complete to a shade with pink ribbons!" Elinor clapped her hands together in delight. The sound made Pallas sidestep and brought Charlie quickly over.

"What are you two laughing about?"

Knowing Charlie to be in danger of dangling after Faith Underhill, Brandley evaded the question. "Just a literary allusion you wouldn't understand."

"Should hope not! That sort of thing can ruin a fellow socially. Bad ton."

"Oh, dear." Elinor's sigh did not cover her amusement. "Have we sunk ourselves quite beyond reproach?"

Miss Rashton, doing her duty as chaperone, turned in her saddle and invited Elinor to ride ahead with the other women.

Elinor joined the tittering Underhill sisters and spent much of the ride to Ranswood giving superficial answers to their chatter.

Lord Widkham met his guests at the foot of the avenue that led to the Ranswood Park manor and escorted them up the broad approach lined with laurels and rhododendrons. The imposing Gothic country house brought raptures of delight from the vicarage girls, who exclaimed over the symmetry of its long windows, the charm of its steep gables, and the variety of its numerous chimneys. Set in the center of a manicured lawn laid out in the style of Capability Brown, the house was magnificent. Its mellow brick walls were covered with trailing ivy, and its leaded windows sparkled with the labor of devoted housemaids.

The party drank lemonade on the flagstone terrace before venturing to the strawberry fields. As the Misses Underhill were simply bursting with enthusiasm to pick berries, it wasn't long before Jack offered his arm to Elinor to lead the way across the magnificent lawn to the field beyond the shrubbery. Charlie appointed himself escort for the vicarage group, leaving Brandley at the back of the party in the role of observer.

As the animated berry-pickers attacked the ripe fruit, Brandley wished he had brought a book. He would rather sit under one of the large shade trees bordering the enclosure and read of Elysian fields.

Just then Elinor rejoined him, dangling a bright red strawberry from its stem. "The plumpest, ripest one I could find. They are so good fresh from the field with the midday sun on them."

Brandley took the berry from her fingers and savored its juicy sweetness.

Lord Widkham had instructed his servants to set the tables, complete with white linen, gleaming silver, and flowered Wedgwood on the lawn under the shade of two ancient elm trees. Soon the party was treated to cold meats, jellies, cheeses, and bread and butter to accompany the crystal bowls of strawberries with their companion pitchers of thick, sweet cream.

Renewed by the meal, the Misses Underhill turned to the marquess and requested to be shown the grounds, and by no means did they wish to miss the pleasure of walking in his extensive woods. And so the party was off once more, strolling through the formal garden, the rose garden, the terraced garden, and even the kitchen herb garden before passing through the herbaceous border and entering the wood. Brandley would have felt pleasure in this had not the attentions of their host to Miss Silbert been so well received by her answering smiles.

When they entered the woods, however, the services of the Lord of Ranswood were required to identify several trees and bushes outside the scope of Miss Rashton's expertise. This gave Elinor the chance to join Brandley. She didn't wait for him to offer his arm, but slipped her hand through his elbow. "It's delightful in the woods on such a warm day. I love that fresh earthy fragrance. Why does it always smell better in the shade?"

They paused to admire a particularly stately evergreen. Then they walked slowly in the shade of the sycamores, laurels, and firs until they came to a widening in the path where a bench had been placed between two lilac bushes. "Oh, let's sit here for a minute." Elinor gathered her skirt to one side of the seat.

Equally glad of her company and the opportunity for a rest, although he would never have admitted it, Brandley complied. Soon they were absorbed in conversation.

It was some time later that Elinor paused and looked around. "Oh, I fear we've lost our party. Do you suppose we shall be missed?"

"Let's try to catch them before the conscientious Miss Rashton comes hunting us." Brandley pushed himself up.

Although they went at a fairly brisk pace in the direction the party had gone, they could not catch a glimpse of them.

"There are so many bypaths. It's impossible to know which way they have gone." Brandley paused at a branching trail. "This path appears to lead back in the direction of the manor. Shall we return and await them in the garden?"

"I daresay that would be the thing to do," Elinor agreed. They walked on for some time in silence, enjoying the lush beauty of the woods and the clear notes of birds' songs. Then Elinor caught sight of a clump of lavender foxgloves growing where the sun broke through a small clearing.

"Brandley, just see!" She ran toward them. In her delight she failed to notice a small rabbit hole almost hidden in the grass. As her foot caught in it, she fell to the ground with a cry of startled pain. Brandley was at her side in a few halting strides.

"Let's have a look at that." He took her ankle gently in his hands and removed her boot. "I've had some experience with this sort of thing." The grim irony in his voice was at odds with the concern in his face.

Elinor gasped when Brandley's examining

fingers touched the pulled ligament. He took his handkerchief from his pocket and expertly wrapped the throbbing ankle. "I'm sure nothing's broken, but it was a nasty wrench, and you'll have to stay off it to keep it from swelling."

"Yes, doctor," she replied meekly with a rather weak smile. "But what are you going to do about my grass-stained gown?"

"Quite beyond my expertise, I fear." He reached for her dislodged hat and brushed it off before returning it to her. "But my more immediate concern is how I'm going to get you back to the house."

Elinor, who had been so relaxed in his understanding care, frowned at their predicament. "Perhaps you should return to the house and send the servants for me."

"I am not willing to leave you here alone. Besides, I'm not at all sure I'd find you again in this infernal maze."

"Then by all means, don't leave me!"

Brandley rose awkwardly from his kneeling position beside her. "Do you think you could get up by yourself?" He held out his hands.

Her reply was to grasp his hands and pull herself up somewhat unsteadily on her uninjured foot. Biting her lip against the pain and still clinging to his hand, she took a tentative hop toward the path. "Oh!" she cried in surprise as a pair of strong arms swept her off her feet and held her firmly at chest level.

"Brandley," she started to protest, "do you think —"

His eyes glinted a determination that silenced her. She meekly put her arm around his shoulders and relaxed.

They were quickly back on the path. "Not too uncomfortable, I hope?" He smiled reassuringly.

"On the contrary, quite the most comfortable stroll in the woods I've ever had." And her smile showed that she meant it.

They had gone on quietly for a few minutes when Elinor gave a soft chuckle. Brandley looked at her in wonder. "I was just thinking what a pair we are!" And she laughed again.

"Oh, I see. You mean the blind leading the blind or more precisely the lame leading the halt." He surprised himself by joining her laughter. "Well, it's a good thing you're so still, or the halt just might not get led at all."

"If that was intended as a warning, it was unnecessary," she said. "I know what happened to Daphne when she struggled against being carried by her Apollo."

"Yes. I remember you mentioned a distinct dislike for leafy arms and bark-covered skin."

Brandley's reply was light, but his left leg increasingly dragged, and a white line appeared around his lips. Conversation was an added effort, so they fell silent. Brandley's common sense valued her thoughtfulness at the same time that his pride resented it. Did she think him such a weakling he couldn't walk and talk at the same time? A halting leg needn't mean a halting tongue. Or was her silence a sign of the scorn he had always known she must feel?

Just then he almost lost his balance as he stepped on the edge of a stick lying in the path, and for a horrifying moment thought he might stumble. He regained his balance, however. Elinor smiled at him quietly. He smiled back, and his appreciation of her serenity banished his angry thoughts. He had grown up accustomed to being thought of as a crippled schoolboy or as "Gwyneth's lame little brother." Having someone rely on him so completely for her welfare was a new and gratifying experience.

In spite of the effort required just to keep walking, Brandley was aware of Elinor in a way he had never been before. He felt her warm breath on his cheek. He smelled her orange-flower-water scent. The feather on her hat tickled his neck. She was so light in his arms, someone fragile to be protected. His arms tightened around her.

Finally the manor house came into sight. Faith Underhill caught sight of them first from the garden and came running and squealing. "Here they are! Oh, Elinor's been hurt!" The rest of the party followed and engulfed the two with their solicitude.

Elinor laughed and protested that their concern was more than she could bear. It went considerably beyond the limit of the exhausted Brandley's endurance. Jack settled Elinor on a garden chaise. Brandley sank stiffly into a chair with a grimace of pain, his face white and shining with perspiration.

Jack ordered a room prepared for Miss Silbert and sent a footman to fetch a doctor. Miss Rashton was full of reproaches to herself for allowing such a thing to happen although it was unclear how she could have prevented it. Faith insisted on regaling the truants with every detail of the search and the fears she had for their safety. Indeed, she appeared more likely to have an attack of the vapors than Elinor, who had already refused Miss Rashton's vinaigrette.

Not to be outdone, Hope managed to ask

Elinor, "Are you in great pain?" and "Can I do something for you?" and "How can you possibly bear up so well?" between every other sentence that was uttered. Charlie made futile attempts to calm the Misses Underhill, who had no wish to be calmed. The appearance of the maid informing Lord Widkham that all was ready rescued Elinor.

Lord Widkham strode commandingly to Elinor, lifted her in his arms, and bore her off toward the house before she had a chance to do more than wave to Brandley. As she turned toward him, sitting a little distance from the noisy group, his strained face changed to a forced smile; but as Lord Widkham had a very quick stride, Elinor was too far across the lawn to speak to him.

The butler announced that tea had been set on the terrace, so they restored themselves while their horses were saddled for the return trip. The heroine of the adventure absent, the Underhills now turned their full attention on its hero. "So courageous of you . . . very difficult. How far did you carry her? You look terribly haggard . . . must be very strong." As the words fell about him, Brandley set his jaw against the pain in his hip and arms. And yet he was aware of a deep satisfaction in what he had managed to do. He hated the pain and fatigue following what would have been merely vigorous exercise to any other man. Yet he had done it.

The next morning, pealing church bells penetrated Brandley's consciousness. His first waking thought was of Elinor. *Is she awake yet? How does she feel?* Then he noticed his own dull headache after a night of very little sleep. *Oh well, we're used to that, aren't we?* He pulled the bell cord for Hollis and lay back on the pillow. Closing his eyes, he remembered how Elinor felt in his arms — until the aroma of coffee announced Hollis's arrival.

"Thank you, Hollis. Just put it on the table."

"Very good, sir." Hollis set the coffee on the table in the center of the room and withdrew.

Well, I'll never know until I try. Brandley gritted his teeth, hoping he could walk. He sat up stiffly and then swung his legs to the floor. Aching muscles made him slow and clumsy, but as he took a deep breath and limped across the floor, he was pleased — he felt quite tolerable. He must be getting stronger. A few years ago yesterday's exertions would have done him in. Hollis returned with hot water, so he washed quickly at the marble stand before drinking his coffee. The hot drink cleared his head, and he began to wonder how soon it would be decent to call at Ranswood Park.

"No, Hollis, not the Hessians — the top boots. I'll be riding this morning."

"Yes, sir." The gyp raised his brows as if to say, *Again today?* but he laid out the appropriate attire.

Brandley surveyed the room — books, papers, quills lying everywhere. "Hollis, my sister and her family are coming tomorrow. Will you see what you can do about this room?"

"Yes, sir. You wish me to clear your desk too?"

"No. I'll see to that later."

Hollis bowed and withdrew. Brandley petted Page idly. Then he decided that if he dressed slowly, it wouldn't be too early to pay a call. He tugged the bell cord again. Hollis appeared in the doorway. "Tell Barrow to saddle Emrys. I'll be down to the stables shortly."

Brandley's exuberance simply would not permit him to stay in his room. He made his way to the stables behind the college along Garret Hostel Lane with as close to a spring in his step as was possible.

In spite of his determination to take his time, a few moments later when the sun burned through the morning mists, he gave Emrys his head, and they raced up Sidney Street. As they passed Holy Trinity Church, he noticed a large crowd of worshipers entering the gates in the high stone wall. He was surprised to see one of his classics professors in the crowd of parishioners and saluted him as he cantered by. *Rackety thing for a don to do — go to church,* he thought. Then he forgot all about it as he urged Emrys along the quickest path to Ranswood Park.

Brandley's arrival could not be too early for Elinor. For some time she had been ensconced on a velvet sofa in a sitting room with numerous pillows at her back and a shawl over her feet. Mrs. Silbert, who had been fetched to Ranswood the night before, had brought Elinor's blue dressing gown with ivory lace at the throat. Elinor was happy to wear it because it accented her blue eyes, a fact she hoped a certain baronet might appreciate should he call on her. And she didn't have long to wait. The book of poetry she held in her hand was still unopened and Mustard no more than settled at her feet when a Ranswood servant ushered in her caller.

"Brandley!" Her eyes lit with a smile.

"How glad I am to see you!" As he crossed the room to take her outstretched hand, she saw that his limp was more pronounced than usual and his pale face still drawn. She noticed too the crisp freshness of his collar points, the precision of his neck cloth, and the trim fit of his long-tailed green riding coat above his polished boots. But more important was the look of confidence she saw in his eyes.

"I didn't get a chance to thank you yesterday. Everything happened so fast." She wanted to tell him that she knew what her rescue had cost him, but she realized he would rather not have it mentioned, so she went on. "Dr. Marston says I'll be up in a few days. And that the injury would have been much worse if I had tried to walk on it. What can I say but thank you, my gallant Apollo?"

Before Brandley could reply to this, Mrs. Silbert came into the room. He dropped Elinor's hand reluctantly to accept her mother's. "I'm so pleased you are here, Sir Brandley. I want to tell you how much my husband and I appreciate the way you took care of our daughter. I'm sure she has told you already that Dr. Marston said the injury might have been quite serious if she hadn't been carried out of the woods."

Again Brandley was unable to reply as this time Jack Widkham entered to make his bow to Mrs. Silbert. Elinor saw Brandley's countenance harden. Jack strode forward with the air of one accustomed to the dominance accorded his rank and presented Elinor with an armful of delicate lavender foxgloves. "And how is our lovely invalid today? I believe these were the guilty parties that led you off the path and into treachery."

"They're beautiful, Jack. Thank you." If her attitude was the least bit cool, neither of her suitors seemed to notice — Jack because of his confidence and Brandley because of his doubt.

"And how are you getting along today, Hilliard?" Jack addressed Brandley without taking his eyes off Elinor.

"I'll do," was Brandley's stiff reply.

"Good. And you, my dear?" Widkham's voice held a note of suave caress. Except for his officiousness, it really was impossible to find much fault with Lord Widkham. The master of a large estate, he had the easy manners that came with great wealth and high breeding. He was a noted sportsman and had a tall, athletic stature. Add to this his dark good looks and passable, if neglected, intelligence.

"Won't you sit down?" Jack said to his

guests and immediately took possession of the chair nearest the sofa. But Brandley declined, giving as an excuse his need to check in at the inn about arrangements for the Calverts' arrival the next day. Without bothering to veil the displeasure in his eyes, Brandley took leave of Elinor and her mother. Then bidding Widkham a cursory farewell, he limped from the room.

6

The Calverts' post chaise and four pulled into the courtyard of The Sun at midday Monday and immediately began disgorging children, servants, and a formidable quantity of portmanteaus and bandboxes. The servants scurried forward at the host's command to carry luggage to the suite reserved for Lord and Lady Calvert.

Lord Calvert and his lady would arrive just enough later to avoid the inevitable dust raised by the first chaise on the deeply rutted roads. The Calverts had elected to travel behind in the barouche, attended only by their groom, Reeth, and two outriders. They enjoyed the fresh air and better view in the open carriage, but more important, it gave them a few moments alone — after several weeks of the London season. Gwyneth, who had been reared not far from the Yorkshire moors, delighted in London's social life; but quiet times like this her soul required. Also, sending the chaise on ahead meant that much of the initial bustle and confusion would be over by the time they arrived.

Gwyneth had but one thought on her mind. She wanted everything settled quickly so she could see to Brandley. She had not for one moment forgotten the topic she had broached with Calvert weeks ago. Her brother was in need of a wife. And it was her duty to do what she could. Her plans for a quick settling in, however, had gone a bit awry. She was greeted by a red-faced host.

"Lady Calvert." The innkeeper gave a jerky bow. "Lord Calvert." This time his bow was accompanied by wringing hands. "To think that it could have happened in my inn." He mopped his forehead with a large white handkerchief. "Let me assure you that everything is being done —"

His muddled apology was cut short by Nana's approach with a wailing Lady Amy in her arms. "Oh, Milady, I turned my back only for a minute."

Lady Calvert took Amy and quieted her while Calvert turned to a servant who had returned for the last of the bandboxes. "You look like a sensible man. What is going on here?"

"It's the young master. He off'd."

"Peter? He's run away?" Gwyneth's voice was sharp.

"He was here. Then he wasn't." The servant picked up four cases and trudged away.

"Calvert . . ." Gwyneth's voice caught on the lump in her throat.

"Don't be alarmed, my dear. The young scamp is absolutely fearless, but he's unlikely to make it to the ends of darkest Cambridgeshire undetected. You carry on with the unpacking. The servants and I will find the boy. And when we do, he won't forget it."

Gwyneth forced her attention to the rooms. She was pleased to find that the beds had been properly aired and that it would not be necessary to unpack the linens they always carried with them. They had chosen The Sun from a list in *The New Cambridge Guide for 1824* of the best accommodations in Cambridge. It was closest to Trinity, and it was where the Duke of Sussex lodged when in Cambridge. But even then one couldn't always be sure.

Relief over the rooms, however, only left her freer to worry about her son. If anything had happened . . .

A clatter on the hardwood stairs sent her running to the door. She pulled back sharply at the sight of her dripping son hanging from his father's arm. "Peter! Oh, Denton, was he in the river?" She grabbed a blanket from the linen basket to cover him.

"Nothing so dramatic. The Renaissance fountain in the middle of Trinity courtyard.

The rascal scrambled up the side and was sailing his boat in it."

Torn between relief and dismay, Gwyneth toweled her son's hair vigorously.

"It sailed great." Then the pert smile faded. "But it got stuck, and I had to go in after it."

"And then the college porter had to go in after you, young man. That fountain supplies the college with drinking water. It is not a paddling pool for imps on holiday. Now apologize to your mother for worrying her. Then you must speak to the landlord and all the others you've inconvenienced."

"I am sorry for worrying you, Mama. I shan't do it again — ever."

The sparkle in his dark eyes left Gwyneth wondering how long "ever" would be. She sent him off to Nana. Now she could instruct Repton to order the tea table laid in their private sitting room and dispatch a messenger to tell Brandley they had arrived. And she could turn her thoughts to designs for her brother's future.

Tea and queenscakes arrived just minutes before Gwyneth heard a dragging step in the hall outside the parlor. She ran to welcome her brother, not waiting for Repton to open the door.

"How are you, my dear?" She was surprised and pleased when he returned her embrace.

He's changed more than I expected. Gwyneth scrutinized him covertly. *It must be the fulfillment of completing his work.*

Gwyneth had changed from her traveling suit to an afternoon frock of embroidered cambric with long sleeves and, in the latest fashion, a band at the natural waistline. She sat at the table and poured their tea.

"I shan't bore you with Lady Bramstoke's charming rout party, Brandley, although you would have been amused by her 'simple' supper. Her cook really outdid himself on the peeper pie. That, in case you lack experience, is newly hatched turkeys put into a pie, to be taken out by spoonfuls. I really much preferred the veal burrs — sweetbreads stuffed with liver, heart, and gizzards of fifty woodcocks. Didn't you, Denton?"

"I assure you, my dear, that choosing between peeper pie and veal burrs exercised me greatly."

"Did anyone inquire into the woodcock's opinion on the matter?" Brandley quizzed his sister.

Fully into the spirit of her story, Gwyneth continued. "But, wait, you really must hear of the most remarkable dish — borne on an enormous silver platter by six footmen. It was composed chiefly of milk, eggs, harts-horn, and currants, I believe," she said, counting them off on her fingers, "molded in the shape of a *hedgehog* and stuck with almond quills and currant eyes."

"A singular dish, to be sure." Brandley handed his empty cup to his sister.

Gwyneth served tea around. Then, watching closely for signs of the new Brandley she sensed under his familiar exterior, she went on. "You truly ought to have been at the opera with us — *Orpheus and Eurydice*. Unfortunately, Gluck ignored the happy wedding and opened act one at the tomb of Eurydice with Orpheus expressing his wild grief." Her pantomime suggested frenzied pulling of hair and flailing of arms, much to her listeners' amusement. "Then Amor tells him he may make the journey into Hades to rescue her, but he must on no account turn to look upon her, or she will be seized by death again.

"Now perhaps you, my learned brother, can explain to me why he should have been willing to descend into Hades to rescue such a ninnyhammer. All the way out she complains that he is indifferent to her — that he has not given her so much as a single glance and that, indeed, without his love she would prefer death. Why does she suppose he risked the powers of Hell and darkness to rescue her? Or when it comes to that, why couldn't he simply have told her Amor required him not to look on her until the rescue was complete? Anyway she got her wish. She badgered him until he turned to reassure her, and she sank to the ground lifeless."

"And so he was forced to return to earth alone in utter desolation," Brandley concluded.

"Certainly not. How can you be so heartless? Amor appeared again and told Orpheus that he had suffered and toiled greatly and so would be forgiven. With a touch he restored Eurydice to life and to her husband's arms."

"A myth with a happy ending? Preposterous. What can Gluck have been thinking of?" Brandley appeared torn by amusement over Gwyneth's account and dismay at the desecration of the myth. The standard version had the disconsolate Orpheus wandering the countryside with his lyre, singing of his lost love until slain by a band of Maenads and buried in a tomb at the foot of Mount Olympus where to this day the nightingales sing more sweetly than anywhere else.

Brandley introduced his own topic now. "You must tell this to a friend of mine. She is studying the tale as an artistic subject."

Eureka! She had unearthed what she had been digging for. Gwyneth leaned forward to hear every word. But the account turned out to be disappointingly cryptic, focusing more on his friend's painting than on the intriguing female herself. But the fact remained — there was a woman in her brother's life. She had never thought to see such animation in her disciplined, scholarly brother. And when she had offered him a dish of strawberries, he had stunned her by mentioning a strawberrying party — without doubt the most frivolous entertainment she had ever known him to attend. She must know more.

"Pray, tell us more of your painter friend."

"Mrs. Silbert?" Brandley took a sip of tea. "Her husband is Master of Peterhouse. Of course, he's much older than she, but she finds much enjoyment in her art."

Denton had finished his tea sometime earlier and was now pacing the room. He turned abruptly. "I hope that groom stabled my cattle adequately. Care to see my new chestnut, Hilliard? A real high-stepper."

Totally oblivious to the sharp looks Gwyneth sent him, Calvert left with Brandley. Lady Calvert sat staring at her cup of cooling tea in horrified astonishment. Brandley — in a liaison with an older married woman? A Master's wife? What could he be thinking of? Quite apart from the unsuitability of the matter, such an affair could ruin his career. She must speak to Denton at once.

Lord Calvert soon returned alone from the stable, his mind at rest, to find his wife in a state of agitation.

"Denton, did Brandley speak to you privately of any, er, attachment he has formed?"

"Attachment?" Denton frowned at his wife. His eyebrows shot up to his hairline. "You don't mean a member of the muslin company? Not Hilliard!" Then his astonishment dissolved into laughter. "What a hoax! I daresay, I took you seriously for a moment."

"Denton, I am not funning."

Lord Calvert struggled manfully to assume a straight face. "My dear, I do hope you are right. But will you never be happy? Only a few weeks ago you were sunk in the dismals over the prospect of his becoming an academic recluse. A bit o' muslin might be the very thing."

"Sir, have you no more propriety than to speak to your wife so? But I must admit that a member of the, er, muslin company, as you put it, might be preferable to a liaison with a married woman."

"What? Fustian! Gwyneth, you must have gotten hold of the wrong end of the stick."

"I have not. He told me so himself. And she's a Master's wife. Denton, do you realize what the scandal could do to his career?"

"I am certain you're mistaken, but I shall undertake to see how far your brother has progressed toward becoming an out-and-out rake."

"Oh, Denton, you don't think —" Then she saw the twinkle in his eye. "Denton! It's odious of you to quiz me. I'm serious. And I mean to learn the truth."

Lady Calvert's desire to explore her brother's personal life, however, had to take second place to the commencement week schedule. Gwyneth and Denton accompanied Brandley to the Senate House where the names of the successful candidates in the examinations were to be announced. Gwyneth held her breath as moderators and examiners read off names of the top-honored wranglers. When they came to Trinity, she didn't have long to wait, for Sir Brandley Hilliard, Bart., was pronounced the first.

She let her breath out with a rush and squeezed her husband's arm.

Charlie congratulated his stairmate enthusiastically, and Lady Calvert invited her brother's friend to join them for dinner at The Sun. There he entertained them with stories of what he had suffered living with a scholar who blocked the door with stacks of books, found it necessary to borrow lamp oil in the middle of the night, and chose to study for exams rather than join in card parties. Not a word, however, about her brother's extracurricular activities. She lay awake long that night making and discarding plans.

And Brandley, across the street in his rooms, was also still awake. His thoughts were much less focused than Gwyneth's. Indeed, it was the vagueness of his disquiet that troubled him. Insomnia over academic matters was not a troubling matter. Now, however, . . .

"Page," he called softly. A sleepy tan head appeared from under his bed as Brandley pulled on his boots. Master and dog slipped quietly from the darkened building, past the porter's lodge, and across Trinity Bridge. In the inky waters of the Cam a few scattered stars found only the dimmest of reflections. Brandley walked slowly without regard to the damage the damp grass would do his highly polished boots.

Page, sensing his master's unrest, trotted companionably at his heels as if to say, *I'm here if you want to talk to me.* But Brandley didn't want to talk. The feeling of discontent was too vague to put into words. The book that was to launch his career was on its way to print. The highest of academic honors for which he had worked were his. But rather than an elation of spirit and sense of fulfillment, he felt only an undefined emptiness and disquiet.

And no matter how successfully he covered such feelings for his sister's sake, they remained unshakable. Perhaps if time permitted, he would talk with Elinor, but her convalescence and his schedule made that unlikely.

The following day Brandley was among the first-class graduates to be honored at a reception for the nobility given by His Royal Highness, the Duke of Gloucester, chancellor of the university. Gwyneth dropped numerous hints, each less veiled than the last, that perhaps Brandley would wish to enlarge their guest list.

"You know the invitation allows Denton, as a peer, to bring as many in his party as he wishes," she urged.

"I'm quite satisfied with the present company, Gwyneth, but you may invite anyone you choose."

Gwyneth sighed with irritation. Then she mounted another attempt. "My love, three gentlemen and only one lady is an awkward number for a party. Don't you know any females I could invite? What about that artist friend of yours? Or is she too, er, bluestocking for the duke's reception?"

Brandley looked up from the paper he was reading and blinked. "What? Mrs. Silbert? Oh, I daresay she may be there. If her husband cares to leave his fireside."

So that was how the land lay! Lady Calvert left the parlor to summon her dresser. She must look her best for an occasion that was to hold she knew not what. "My rose sarcenet, Burney," she directed.

The servant produced a gown made in the latest fashion with a wide neckline, long sleeves puffed at the top, and a wide skirt trimmed with a double pleating of ribbon. A short time later, the three deep pink ostrich plumes held in place high on Milady's head by a shining clasp drew a compliment from Lord Calvert as he opened the inn door for her.

As for most of the events of the week,

Lord Calvert wore his nobleman's robes over his formal attire. Unlike most of his peers who went about in all the colors of the rainbow, however, Calvert had chosen sedate black robes trimmed with bands of ermine.

Brandley joined them outside the Great Gate of Trinity. He had no trouble keeping his academic gown in obedient folds over his cream satin knee breeches, white silk hose, black long-tailed coat, and double-breasted silk waistcoat. Charlie, however, who made the third man in the party, was lucky to keep his unruly gown on his shoulders at all.

The room in the Senate House was a squeeze of elegantly dressed guests to be presented to His Royal Highness, William Frederick, Duke of Gloucester. Gwyneth eagerly looked forward to meeting this notorious member of the royal family.

"I wonder what he's like, Denton. Could he really be as dim-witted as *Figaro* makes him out to be?"

"It's unlikely. You know how *Figaro* always scoffs at rank and royalty."

"Yes, but it's more than that. Of course, all his charities are fine, I suppose, but what about his being an Evangelical? If that's true, it's no wonder they question his election as

Chancellor of Cambridge. And what about this Charles Simeon and his evangelical friends? They say they're making simply drastic changes in the religious life of the school."

Whatever the level of his intellect or acceptance might be, however, the Duke of Gloucester was a royal. And it was well worth standing in line for over an hour to be presented to him.

The receiving line moved slowly as each guest's name was presented to the chancellor by a page who stood at his side. "The Viscount and Viscountess Calvert, Your Royal Highness." Gwyneth held out her hand, curtsied deeply, and looked up into the duke's lusterless but kind, wide, round eyes. She gave him her sweetest smile and was surprised at how his almost ugly face turned merry when he returned her smile. *Poor man,* she thought, *nature must have been in a whimsical mood when she made this prince.* The line moved on.

From the receiving line the guests moved to a long table laden with gourmet delights set out on graduated terraces ornamented by ice carvings of swans and dolphins. A three-tiered gold-plated fountain bubbled with wine, which then ran the length of the table in a little rivulet floating with gardenias.

Gwyneth moved slowly past the stunning array of dishes — exquisitely garnished galantines, gelees, and glacees. She chose a small serving of galantine of duck and then a ground mixture of duck with pork and veal flecked with truffles, pistachio nuts, and ham served on a glistening tray en gelee. An elegant chartreuse was next — custard of pureed vegetables molded in a colorful mosaic of alternating rows of vegetables precisely cut and arranged in a complex design.

It was difficult to take only a small helping of the pheasant Souvaroff. The succulent bird had been roasted in a pastry crust with truffles and *foie gras* and served with a Burgundy sauce. Next, a pheasant in its splendid plumage watched over a covey of quail breasts also stuffed with *foie gras* and truffles and coated with aspic. Gwyneth simply forced herself to close her eyes to the next assortment of dishes presented to tantalize the palate, but she could not resist the miniature birds fashioned of pigeon breasts and grapes.

Because of the warmth of the evening, small round tables had been set on the stone courtyard. Potted shrubs were interspersed among the tables, giving a sense of privacy where in actuality none existed. The Calvert party soon found their private conversation interrupted by voices which carried all too well on the evening air. After an uncomfortable attempt to ignore the intruding voices, they gave their attention to their food.

"I thought of that line from Dryden, 'and lambent dullness plays around his face,' " remarked a nasal male voice. The unkind witticism at the expense of the Duke of Gloucester drew peals of laughter from the speaker's companions.

"But, my dear," a shrill female voice said above the laughter, "how is it possible that a royal duke could be aligned with those Evangelicals? I am told they espouse *enthusiasm* in one's religion."

"It is shocking, but with such notable personages as the Duchess of Beaufort, William Wilberforce, and even Lord Harrowby on their side, it is difficult for right-minded people to attack their gospel-preaching ministry and Sunday schools and other such subversion in the established church."

It seemed to the captive listeners that everyone at the next table began talking at once about the evangelical excesses they felt the Duke of Gloucester symbolized: "Circulating the Bible without the prayer book will undoubtedly encourage the growth of dissent. And the Church Missionary Society collaborates with dissenters. . . . But, my dear, our vicar, a most respectable type, I assure you, told me one of them even wants to establish missions in *India*."

The young man with the nasal voice returned to his earlier theme. "The latest on dit is that Silly Billy complained that the flies kept getting in his mouth when he was out riding last week. His groom is said to have replied, 'Perhaps Your Royal Highness had better shut your mouth.' "

Gwyneth shifted uncomfortably on her chair. She was glad that the long windows of the Senate House were closed so that the duke could not hear. Much to her relief, the sound of wood scraping on the stone heralded the noisy party's departure. As they passed the Calverts' table, Gwyneth recognized the strikingly beautiful woman in the group. Her tall, lithe figure was exquisite in a garnet silk dress with a low neckline and puffed sleeves that admirably set off her white shoulders. A black velvet bow emphasized her tiny waistline. Festoons of silk flowers around a fashionably short hemline called attention to a pair of trim ankles, just as clusters of the same flowers arranged in her intricate coiffure drew one's eye to an abundance of shining auburn tresses.

The lady started to sweep past in queenly

fashion when her eye caught Lord Calvert, and she stopped to offer a delicate lace-mitted hand to him. Rising swiftly, Calvert bowed over the hand and presented the beauty to the others. "Lady Ormsby, I believe you met Lady Calvert at Lady Bramstoke's rout party; and may I present my brother-in-law, Sir Brandley Hilliard, and his friend, Mr. Verdun." The gentlemen barely had time to make their bows before Lady Ormsby was claimed by her party. But not before the full radiance of her smile had rested on Sir Brandley.

Charlie was still staring at the path the woman had taken. "Charles seems much taken by the Alluring Lurinda." Gwyneth smiled with amusement.

As if coming out of a trance, Charlie shook his head slowly. "Who was she?"

"The Lady Lurinda Ormsby, the *Ne Plus Ultra*," Calvert replied. "Every season has its Incomparable, but there has been only one *Ne Plus Ultra*."

"What is she doing in Cambridge?" Charlie seemed to be visibly restraining himself from tugging at his neck cloth.

"I believe she has a brother graduating," Calvert said.

Brandley nodded. "The fellow with the nasal voice. He's at St. John's."

But Gwyneth's mind was not on her London acquaintance. "They were too hard by half on the duke." She recalled the flash of charm she had seen in the shy, awkward man. "His appearance is that of a gentleman, if not quite betokening a man of princely rank."

"However that may be, love, his statements are singular." Denton finished a last morsel of pears in frangipani cream. "On hearing that the army intended to abolish corporal punishment, he is said to have remarked that he would give the project his support as he had always thought it hard that only the corporals were flogged."

"It's impossible to tell whether he is not normally bright or whether his hearers are too dense to appreciate his humor. I recall hearing of the time the duke asked how boats were moved, and he was told that it was by means of men who put their sculls into the water. 'Bless my soul,' he replied, 'I have put my skull into my washbasin at least a hundred times, and I have never moved an inch.'"

When the laughter subsided, they began to go over the events scheduled for the week. A concert followed the reception, and an oratorio would be performed tomorrow — Bach's *St. Matthew's Passion*, Brandley thought, or was it *St. John's*? They looked forward to another concert on the afternoon of the following day. That night Brandley's attendance would be required at the annual sermon preached at Great St. Mary's for the benefit of Addenbrooke Hospital, one of the duke's numerous charities. Saturday they would attend the Midsummer Faire on Midsummer Common along the river. Commencement Sunday would bring the preaching of the university sermon, attendance again mandatory. Then it was traditional for the whole academic world to spend half an hour walking up and down on Clare Hall Place, the green space in front of Clare College, the academicians exhibiting their colorful robes and the women admiring and being admired in their best frocks. Monday would bring two congregations — one at eleven o'clock in the morning, the other at two in the afternoon. That day's events were to be capped by the annual Commencement Ball, for which Charlie informed his listeners that Miss Underhill had already promised him the dinner dance. The next day came graduation.

Charlie was so overcome by the outline of such an exhausting schedule that he went off to refill his plate and build his energy for the week. But Gwyneth could extract no information from her brother regarding any arrangements he had made for female companionship, which strengthened her suspicions that the attachment was improper.

7

As the week sped by in frantic activity, Brandley found no time to call on Professor Silbert to learn of Elinor's convalescence nor to visit her at Ranswood. But whenever he had a quiet moment he thought of her; and when he closed his eyes after a tiring day, the vision of her on the sofa, smiling at him and holding out her hand to him, filled his mind.

But for some reason he did not speak to Gwyneth of her. Perhaps it was simply because he had let it go so long that now it would be impossible to introduce the topic in a casual manner. Or perhaps it was because he was uncertain how to express his feelings. Or perhaps it was because each time he pictured her in his mind, the vision blurred with the entrance of Lord Widkham.

With increasing frustration, Brandley fought against his inability to alter that vision. He doubted that he would have chosen to squelch his feelings for Elinor if such a course had been within his power, but any attempt to define them seemed futile. He searched his classical knowledge for a story or poem, but found none that expressed his own emotions. And as social and academic events filled every moment, he was unable to vie for a place in her attentions to erase Lord Widkham's picture from the scene.

Commencement Sunday was a cloudless blue and yellow June day that would have been perfect for exercising Emrys on the fields behind Peterhouse or for driving to Ranswood to see if Elinor were well enough to take the air in his phaeton. But attendance at the university sermon was mandatory, so Brandley escorted his relatives to the event.

The sermon was to be preached by one of those controversial supporters of the Duke of Gloucester — the noted and sometimes notorious King's fellow, Charles Simeon, who was also vicar of Holy Trinity Church.

"I saw a large and varied crowd in front of his church while riding by on Sunday morning recently," Brandley mentioned.

"Seems to me there was some controversy surrounding Simeon's appointment to Holy Trinity. Yet he drew large crowds even when the regular pew-holders fixed locks on their pews in protest." Calvert kept abreast of political and ecclesiastical controversies.

Brandley paused as they crossed King's Parade and neared Great St. Mary's, the university church. "But why should they have protested at all? I believe he's very venerated now — not quite in my line of interest, of course — but hardly a figure to rouse the rabble."

"That was many years ago. I recollect he was only in his twenties, rather before my time. But the chief complaint wasn't his lack of expertise in the pulpit. It was his vehemence in preaching the gospel."

Gwyneth registered surprise. "Denton! You don't mean to say that we are to hear a *Methodist* preach the college sermon, do you?"

Denton laughed. "Have no fear, my love. The old gentleman is quite soundly Anglican. To preach before the university is, in academic circles, to have arrived. And I understand the honor has been conferred upon Simeon nearly ten times."

"What a fount of information you are." Lady Calvert preceded her escorts through the dark carved doors of Great St. Mary's.

The congregation was talking, whispering, and gazing about them. In spite of Simeon's reputation as a powerful preacher, apparently many of them were prepared to scorn or to scrape — that tiresome undergraduate custom of showing disapproval or boredom by shuffling their feet on the floor. Sir Brandley and the Calverts took seats in a box pew near the front reserved for the nobility

118

in the midst of dons, masters, and under-graduates.

Brandley looked around the dimly lit church. The few rays of sun that made their way through the high, traceried windows did little to illuminate the dark carved woods and gray stone floors and walls. He had no intention of engaging in anything as discourteous as scraping, but his barely stifled yawn showed how little he expected. Compulsory chapel twice daily was more than enough trial to be borne in the name of religion. Sunday sermons went beyond all bounds.

But as the ringing of changes ceased to resound from the belfry above and the echoes died high in the vaulted roof, the congregation quieted at the entrance of the preacher.

Led with dignity by a sexton in a gown adorned with gold lace, Simeon, in a voluminous white surplice with hood and black scarf, walked to the altar and knelt in prayer. A hush fell on the audience. As he rose and went to the reading desk, the congregation slipped to their knees. At first Brandley couldn't figure out what was different. He had listened to prayers being read from the prayer book almost every day for three years. Then he realized — for the first time he could hear the words; he could hear the prayers actually being prayed as an act of worship. It was almost as if this were heart-felt supplication to a real God — not an ode chanted to the clouds.

As the service continued, the preacher seemed so intensely aware of the presence of God that he was able to infuse the whole congregation with a feeling of solemn devotion.

After the choir sang a hymn, Simeon disappeared from view as he climbed the hidden staircase. He emerged a moment later in the great oak pulpit at the west end of the sanctuary. Spreading out his sheets of sermon notes on the pink cushion with its tasseled corners, he looked out on the congregation. As he began to preach, not a gownsman moved his feet. In the atmosphere of the moment, Brandley thought of Goldsmith's parson who preached so that:

Truth from his lips prevail'd with double sway,
and fools, who came to scoff, remain'd to pray.

It was not that Brandley himself accepted all in the sermon as truth, but that the speaker so earnestly believed it to be so made it impossible to scoff. Brandley contemplated the victory the years had won for this protagonist of the Word of God — from preaching to a nearly empty church with locked pews to filling the most honored pulpit in the city before a congregation so large that extra chairs had to be put in the aisles.

Afterward, Brandley remembered little of the sermon topic or exposition, but the remarkable spirit of the man who filled the pulpit remained with him as a disturbing presence.

Monday afternoon the second congregation assembled for the reading of the members' prizes. To no one's surprise but his own and much to everyone's pleasure, Brandley received a gold medal for the best dissertation in Latin prose.

But one honor Brandley didn't win — indeed he would have been embarrassed if he had — was the cash award for universal chapel attendance. Nor did he see any laurels in this category going to members of Charlie's Prevention of Cruelty to Undergraduates Society. It amazed him that any had the piety and stamina to earn such an award.

A ball followed the awards, which held no interest for Brandley; so after wishing his anxious stairmate well, he offered to take his nephew and brother-in-law on a tour of the campus. Peter was full of self-importance. He wore his best suit — buff pantaloons and a short brown jacket with two rows of brass buttons. The round white collar of his shirt framed his animated face and golden brown curls, giving an angelic look to the little imp, who was completely heartless at leaving his sister behind wailing, "Take Amy too!"

"Nah, baby girls can't go. This is for men."

Amy felt better when "Unca Bwany" ruffled her black curls, wiped her tears, and presented her with a sweet, accompanied by a promise that she should have a ride in his phaeton later — just the two of them — if Nana approved.

Peter exclaimed over the gargoyles adorning the front of King's College Chapel, but once inside he soon grew bored. For a few minutes he played tag with the crimson, blue, and green patches projected from the stained glass onto the floor. Then he wandered about the great nave, apparently wishing he could climb one of the arches to touch the spreading fans of white stone. Soon his neck began to ache from so much looking up. He did the only practical thing — he lay on his back on the stone floor.

"The stained-glass windows," Brandley explained to Denton, "were made by English and Flemish artisans working in England in the sixteenth century. They were considered the best example of Flemish Renaissance glass-painting in existence." Denton examined the exquisite detail of the figure of the Virgin Mary.

Brandley looked around. "Where's Peter?"

Calvert shook his head. "We should never have let him out of leading strings. We call him the heir unapparent. The scamp constantly has the household at sixes and sevens." In a moment, however, a giggle came from behind the carved rood screen. Recovering the truant, they continued the tour.

They walked along the path lined with King James's elms leading from King's to the Backs. Then a thought made Peter brighten. "Did you know they're going to dig a tunnel under the Thames, Uncle?"

"Well, that's fine, but as we have no tunnels under the Cam, you'll have to make do with our bridges."

There were many strollers on the Backs that day promenading beside the placid green waters. A girl with golden curls passed by on the arm of her companion, and Brandley caught his breath. Of course, it wasn't Elinor, but the sight increased the ache of her absence.

When the three reached the promised bridge, Brandley and Denton waited with uncharacteristic patience, waving to Peter as he appeared between each of the traceried, Gothic-arched grids. While responding to yet another command to "Look!" Brandley caught sight of a familiar figure emerging from St. John's library and crossing the bridge. As the don reached the uppermost curve of the bridge, a puff of wind caught his black robe, making it billow out like a giant crow ready to take flight.

"Doctor Silbert," Brandley greeted him as the professor drew near. "Allow me to present my brother-in-law, Lord Calvert. Denton, it is Mrs. Silbert who is doing a painting on the Orpheus and Eurydice subject."

"I wish I could invite you to visit us," Dr. Silbert said. "But my wife has taken a slight cold and will probably be unable even to attend commencement exercises."

"That is a disappointment to all of us, sir." Calvert offered a small bow. "Please convey our wish for her speedy recovery."

"How is Elinor, sir?" Brandley asked.

Calvert raised his eyebrows at this casual use of a Christian name.

"Chafing at her enforced inactivity." The don shook his head. "Dr. Marston is satisfied with her progress, but he refuses to let her off the sofa for at least two more days. These things are best left to time, you know."

Brandley did know. Mentally, he saw Elinor confined for those two more days while Jack plied her with flowers and Brandley played host to his guests and attended compulsory functions. His slowed step was accompanied by a grim expression as they walked back to the inn.

Gwyneth was dressing for dinner that evening when her husband knocked on the dressing room door. Calvert watched with a gleam in his eye as Burney finished brushing my lady's golden curls and picked up a small cap of Belgian lace. "No, no. Must you wear that thing? It hides your curls."

Gwyneth laughed. "It's a small cap and very fashionable." But she signaled for Burney to put the cap away and withdraw. "And now I'm on tenterhooks to know the cause of that cat-with-the-cream look you're wearing."

"I have to report, my dear, that you may not be making the piece of work about nothing that I believed you to be. I have just met our elusive Dr. Silbert."

"The artist's husband? Pray, what is he like?"

"Short, bald, bookish —"

"Indeed, just the man to bore a high-spirited wife? I was convinced I wasn't being caper-witted in this. What are we to do, Denton? Did you learn anything more about her?"

"Only that her name is Elinor and that your brother uses her Christian name to her husband's face."

"As bad as that? Denton, what *are* we to do?"

"Do? Why, nothing."

"But, Denton, it's not a proper way to behave."

"On the contrary, it's quite the thing in the most fashionable circles. Wherever did you contract such Methodist morals?"

"Odious creature! I am quite sunk to think that my husband and my brother could be such shabsters. But if you won't do anything, at least I can take care to keep Brandley fully engaged for the next days and out of the grasp of that conniving female."

"Or her out of his?" Denton returned with a wicked chuckle.

8

On the morning of commencement day, the parson's bell at St. Mary's began pealing at 5:45 and continued for fifteen minutes to awake the bed-makers and gyps, who in turn roused their charges to prepare for the day. Before long, the campus came alive, and the college walks were crowded. The doctors in the university wore their scarlet robes while the noblemen appeared in splendid gowns of purple, white, green, or rose. Townspeople and some from neighboring villages, not daring to venture past the rails separating the walks from the high road, crowded to the railings to peer through at the colorful spectacle.

Brandley had gone earlier to the courtyard outside the Senate House. There he received a printed copy of the forms to be observed by all commencers and was shown his place in the march by a bedell, who would then walk at the head of the procession.

Charlie came a bit early for Lord and Lady Calvert so that they might arrive at the Senate House in time to secure good seats. As they took their places in the rapidly filling room, Gwyneth admired the symmetry of the building, elegantly ornamented with wainscots, statues, and carved oak galleries. The gallery at the upper end of the room was crowned with a pediment supported by four Doric columns of beautifully carved oak. Under the pediment on raised steps was the vice-chancellor's chair, and on each side were semicircular seats for the masters and doctors.

Charlie pointed out the statue of King George I on the north wall, King George II on the opposite wall, and he would have gone on to name all the statues lining the walls, but at that moment the strains of regal music by Handel filled the room. The academic procession began.

King's entered first because of its royal charter, followed by Trinity and St. John's, also with royal privileges. The other colleges followed in the order of their founding — Peterhouse, the oldest, leading the rest. The congregation stood as the procession passed slowly across the black and white marble floor.

Brandley, as senior wrangler, marched at the head of his college, tall and solemn. Gwyneth saw the gleam of determination in his eye and knew with an ache in her throat that he was trying very hard not to limp. Her eyes misted over as she felt a surge of pride. She saw him as a boy of ten, ignoring the pain in his frail body, his delicate face frowning with concentration at his tutor's explanation of a difficult theorem. She remembered how he held heavy volumes until his arms ached. She recalled the turning point when he could sit a horse and go to what he called his "serious study" with Dr. Midgeholme, their vicar. It was Dr. Midgeholme who had inspired the boy with the confidence to succeed and who had sent him to Cambridge far better prepared than if he had gone to Eaton as he had desired. The fact that he was several years older than many of his Trinity classmates had also helped.

After the commencers took their places and the congregation was seated, the impressive ceremony, unchanged since medieval times, began. As the names of the King's graduates were called in order of their academic standing, a movement from the students leaning over the railing of the gallery caught Gwyneth's eye. She glanced upward and was surprised to see a rope hanging from one balcony to the other. Throughout the ceremony it continued there, slack and meek.

Finally the list of King's graduates neared the end. As the name of the last student was called and he rose — lowest-ranking scholar in his class — a huge wooden spoon resembling an oar was let down on the balcony rope to the accompaniment of jeers, whistles, and catcalls.

This hapless commencer had the unhappy distinction of being wooden spoon — the extreme opposite of senior wrangler. Blushing and grinning sheepishly, he made his way forward with the spoon, but the look on his face said that he wished he had spent less time at wine and card parties and more time studying.

Charlie seemed to take the lesson to heart. He muttered, "Must attend lectures more next year. Maybe I can arrange a schedule that starts later in the day."

When Trinity's turn came to receive their degrees, Brandley, as senior wrangler, was among the first four to be presented. The praelector extended four fingers to them. Each graduate grasped a finger in his right hand, to be led to the vice-chancellor. The praelector paused, bowed with his cap raised, and three times announced his sons fit to receive their degrees. Brandley was the first to kneel, placing his hands between those of the vice-chancellor, who pronounced the traditional formula in Latin.

Charlie translated for Gwyneth, "It's

something like, 'I commission you to be admitted to the degree of Bachelor of Arts, in the name of the Father, Son, and Holy Spirit.' Afraid I never was very good at Latin."

But it sounded quite good enough to Gwyneth. She had caught the look of gratification on her brother's face as he returned to his seat.

The rituals over, the family turned their attention to packing Brandley's belongings. The day before he was to leave, all was a bedlam of trunks, bandboxes, and portmanteaus. Lady Calvert became so impatient directing the servants that she borrowed an apron from Burney and took a hand in the work herself.

She knelt before a veritable mountain of textbooks, notebooks, and hornbooks. "Brandley, are you sure you need *all* these just for the summer?"

"I'm just taking the ones Denton doesn't have in his library." He picked up a heavy stack and placed them in a trunk.

Gwyneth shook her head in amused surrender. "I know, just light recreation."

Charlie bounded in with characteristic abandon, his corgis at his heels. "I say, I'll miss you, Hilliard. Won't be the same trying to walk across a room that's not an obstacle course of books."

Affectionately pulling Chloe's ears, Brandley thought how glad he and Page would be to see his own hunters again. "But you plan to visit your cousin at York this summer, don't you? You can come stumble over my books at Okeford any time you like."

"Rely on it. I hear there's good sport in your country." On that cheerful note, Charlie and the corgis added to the confusion by insisting on lending a hand with the packing — with much good will but little productivity. It was some time later that Chloe was discovered to have chewed a corner off the largest of the rush baskets in which Brandley's linen had been stored. Dismayed at being scolded, she took up a post at the window and howled at the dogs passing in the street below. At this Charlie bade his friends goodbye and dragged his dogs from the room.

By late afternoon the last trunk had been marked and stored for Brandley's return in the fall. Brandley and Calvert supervised the delivery of his summer necessaries to the stage office to be sent by post to Harrogate, and Brandley at last found time to go round to the Silberts to bid his friends farewell. He had thought there would be time sooner, but it seemed Gwyneth had something requiring his attention every moment of the past days.

"You'll find Miss Elinor in the garden, sir," a beaming Katy informed him. "Just back from Ranswood today; Dr. Marston pronounced her fit as a fiddle. It's happy to see you, she'll be, sir."

So elated by this news that his step was almost bouncy, Brandley went around the house by the side path, visions of the fulfillment of this long-awaited moment filling his mind. His hand was still on the latch when he froze in mid-motion of swinging the gate open. Laughing voices told him that, indeed, Elinor was in the garden, but she was not alone.

She and Jack were absorbed in each other's company. Immobilized by the pain that increased every time he saw Jack and Elinor together, Brandley stood woodenly. They sat on the bench at the far end of the garden — the bench where Elinor had invited him to sit with her when he first talked to her about his lameness. Everything about the scene in front of him recalled a memory. Elinor was wearing the jonquil muslin dress she had worn the day of the storm when she first called him her Apollo. She looked like a sun goddess herself today, sitting near a bed of yellow and orange marigolds. She was looking up into Jack's face laughing. The scene was intimate. Interrupting them would be unthinkable. Feeling sick and angry, Brandley silently backed out the half-open gate and strode around the side of the house.

His first thought was simply to leave, but as the path went past the side door that opened into the library, he reconsidered. Dr. Silbert answered his knock. Again he met painful memories. The room recalled scenes of firelight reflected in rich paneling and in Elinor's blue eyes smiling at him. Through clenched teeth he issued a stiff farewell speech to his friend.

"Leaving in the morning, are you?" The professor placed a hand on Brandley's shoulder. "I'll miss you, son."

Brandley winced.

"Well, we hope to get off in a week or so ourselves. I'm very anxious to get on with my research on the duchess."

Brandley requested the professor to convey his farewell to Mrs. Silbert, bowed, and departed.

Gathering his reins, he peremptorily kicked Emrys to a canter and arrived at The Sun, anxious to leave Cambridge and its memories. Only his unusually pale countenance and grimly set mouth hinted at his pain. He gritted his teeth in the same manner he had learned to do against another kind of pain long ago.

For the length of their journey to Okeford, Brandley alternately thought of Elinor and determined to put her out of his mind. He should have interrupted Jack's addresses to her; he shouldn't have gone to the Silberts at all. He wished her happiness, even with Jack; he wished Jack at Jericho. He would probably never see her again, and good work of it too; he missed her terribly. The irony of the situation was that the very act of determining not to think of Elinor required thinking of her.

9

It was good to be back at Okeford, away from the perplexities of Cambridge. Brandley found solace in riding all his favorite lanes, fishing for trout in nearby streams (taking a book along, as always), hunting pheasant in the field, and finding literary treasures in the library. As in days past, he enjoyed long visits with Dr. Midgeholme. The old tutor was justly proud of his pupil's achievement, but he refused to take any of the credit.

On his second day home, Brandley's pointer presented him with a litter of puppies. The squirming, whimpering, white and brown mass delighted Amy and Peter. Amy loved to stroke their soft bellies with just one finger and never tired of smelling the warm milk and hair and watching them suckle. Brandley and Peter spent a happy hour selecting names for them. Peter had been enchanted with his uncle's retelling of the tales of King Arthur, so the pups were named Lance, Uther, Galahad (the almost white one), Balan and Balin (the two who looked most alike), Ulfis (the smallest one), Elaine, Gwen ("But not for my mother," Peter explained), and Merlin (with the starlike spot on his head). Then Brandley thought how delighted Elinor might be with the puppies, and the ache returned.

She would be enchanted with Okeford too, he thought. Visitors were always struck by the elegance of its design — tall rows of perfectly proportioned windows framed by shutters, two dormers between steep stone gables, single-storied rooms at each end opening onto the lawn through French windows (library at one end, music room at the other), festoons of wisteria with pendulous purple blossoms enlivening the brownish-gray stone. Yes, he would have liked to stroll on the lawn with Elinor.

In the evenings he told stories to Amy and roughhoused with Peter before Nana took the children to bed. Then he and Gwyneth and Calvert would have dinner, play chess or cribbage or billiards, and enjoy long talks together. It was so pleasant that he almost forgot the pain of his last night in Cambridge.

Brandley was something of a celebrity in their quiet neighborhood of North Riding. Okeford's nearest neighbors, Edmund and Harriet Ludlow, invited the Okeford family to a dinner party. The host was sufficiently impressed by the scholar's achievement that for the first time in his life, Edmund refrained from treating Brandley with condescending kindness. Brandley had stiffened when the company rose to go into dinner, recalling unwanted assistance from earlier days. When no solicitous hand took his arm to help him out of his chair, he smiled to himself with relief and pulled himself up smoothly.

Much to his surprise, Brandley even found restrained pleasure in his brother's company — Carleton the soldier, the sportsman, the agriculturist. Four years after Waterloo, Carleton had been captivated by a wealth of black ringlets and dancing blue eyes belonging to an officer's daughter. He sold his commission and brought Amelia home to Fancourt where he managed the family estate in Brandley's behalf. The young bride was uncomfortable with her new brother-in-law's intellect and embarrassed by his disability. But Brandley had already made his home with Gwyneth and Denton and then had gone to Cambridge, sparing her the discomfort of his presence.

Despite his lack of comprehension of Brandley's accomplishments, Carleton could not have been prouder of his brother. And Brandley was pleased by the improved relationship. So pleased, in fact, that he was willing to brave an evening in his sister-in-law Amelia's company after Carleton rode over to Okeford to extend his wife's invitation.

"Nothing formal, you understand. With little John just two months old, she's not much away from the nursery yet."

Driving up the lane to Fancourt, Brandley gazed at his childhood home for the first time after many years. He was surprised. He remembered it as much larger. It had been in the Hilliard family for almost 170 years. Charles II had presented it to their ancestor as a reward for their support at the Restoration. The king had signed the writ of deed with his own hand when he created the first Baronet Hilliard.

Compared to Okeford or Ranswood, it was a small country estate, but it looked comfortable with Virginia creeper growing over its red brick walls and around its white-framed windows.

As soon as the guests entered the low wall that surrounded the front garden, they were greeted by Grimsby, their old family butler. "May I say, Sir Brandley, how very glad I am to see you again and to hear of your success."

"Thank you, Grimsby."

Suddenly Nurse bustled in, engulfed the

baronet in her comfortable arms, and crooned in her broad Yorkshire dialect, "Land sakes, Mester Brandley, right proud as I am of my little lamb. Such a successful scholar, that tha'rt. But now tha'll be living in Cambridge permanent, and us'll never see thee. My, but tha'rt still thin as a wisp. Tha' knowest what the Good Book ses, 'Of much studying there is great weariness.' "

Smiling at this beloved, familiar figure, Brandley returned her embrace. "But, Nurse, 'You shall know the truth, and the truth shall make you free.' " That had been the first reply that had come to him when Nurse turned Biblical, but he wondered how appropriate it was. Was he freer with his increased knowledge? The question surprised him. Certainly no classical scholar could ignore Socrates' advice, "Know thyself." With all his academic achievement, did he know himself?

But Carleton was there to take his guests into the parlor where Amelia waited. Beyond adding some highly sentimental paintings of romantic ruins and replacing their mother's rose damask draperies with floral prints, Amelia had left the room unchanged. The Aubusson carpet and Sheraton furniture their mother had chosen as a young bride were still lovely. Amelia had directed the servants to place bowls of roses on the tables at each end of the sofa, and their fragrance mingled with the smell of Carleton's cheroot and the odor of his dogs, which he allowed into the parlor over his wife's protests.

Amelia, wearing an unfashionable profusion of ruffles and curls, sat on the sofa — the same sofa Brandley had spent so much time on as an invalid. Gwyneth held her breath, but Brandley had foreseen the awkward moment. He came forward and bowed slightly to her. "My dear sister-in-law, my brother tells me you have presented him with a third handsome son. May I offer my congratulations." His voice was direct and assured.

Fortunately, Brandley wasn't the only one who had done some maturing. Amelia looked right at him and offered her hand. Gwyneth relaxed visibly.

From then on the evening went smoothly through the soup, trout, aspic, roast mutton with potatoes, and syllabub.

"Gwyneth, dear," Amelia gushed, "I do so wish you could have seen Belinda and Sarah in their bath. You have no idea how bright they are. Why, Sarah splashed so hard I was simply soaked. They are such angels."

"I tell you, Denton," urged Carleton, "you must come over to watch the operation of my new Tull seed drill. It will plant an acre with two pounds of seed instead of the nine or ten pounds required to hand-broadcast."

". . . and I know Brandley will be glad to know what an interest Felix is already taking in the estate even at his early age because, of course, if Brandley doesn't choose to produce an heir himself . . ."

"Now this remarkable invention will make the channels, sow the seed, and cover the rows, all in one operation."

"Do let me pour you some more tea. Oh, is it getting cool? Oh, well, it's not actually cold yet, is it? I see no reason to waste perfectly good tea. I always tell Carleton we must manage the estate just as if it were actually his because, after all, you never know."

"How lucky. I just happen to have a copy of Tull's *Horse-Hoeing Husbandry* to hand. Let me read to you . . ."

". . . and when Felix pulled her curls Belinda said . . ."

Denton, who had been using a horse hoe and seed drill for many years on his estate, barely managed to stifle his yawns. It all came to an abrupt end with a precipitous demand from Amelia that Carleton remove his dogs from the room. The hapless creatures were dragged from in front of the fire, and the Okeford family made their escape from the family circle.

The following week Mrs. Ashperton, Harriet Ludlow's mother, gave an even larger party than the one hosted by Edmund and Harriet. Not that she was competing with her own daughter, goodness knows! But, after all, she was the Hilliard family's oldest friend. This was quite apart, of course, from the fact that she still had an unmarried daughter at home. Brandley found his new social success mildly amusing. Certainly being a sought-after guest of honor was more pleasant than being Lady Calvert's embarrassing encumbrance. And Croydon, the manservant Brandley had hired in keeping with his new position, reveled in turning his new master out in top-of-the-trees fashion for neighborhood social events.

All the North Riding notables Lady Ashperton could make room for gathered in her dining salon. The long table groaned under the weight of a silver epergne piled high and overflowing with flowers, fruit, nuts, and sweetmeats. The ornate arrangement, while marking the festivity of the occasion, blocked any interchange with guests on the other side of the table. Therefore, Brandley, seated at Mrs. Ashperton's right, found himself trapped between the effusions of his hostess and the giggles of her seventeen-year-old daughter, Clara.

"Oh, Sir Brandley, such a powerful intellect fills me with admiration." She flitted her fan in the space between them.

Brandley inclined his head in acknowledgment but leaned away from the threatening fan.

Clara, obviously picturing herself the heroine of the evening, was undeterred by her hero's silence. A devoted reader of romantic novels, she could imagine herself running through the night to keep a tryst with him, her long cape flowing behind her in the moonlight.

"Did you know I'm out, Sir Brandley?"

He blinked. "You're what?"

"I'm out." He would assuredly beg the honor of escorting her to the next neighborhood fete.

"Oh. I am sorry. Out where?"

Taking this to be the height of wit, she gave him her most charming twitter. "You mock me, sir. I made my come-out at mama's cotillion ball last month. And next season I'm to go to London. Papa says I'm to have seven new ball gowns. Isn't that simply prodigious!"

The hero assented.

"Have *you* been to London, Sir Brandley?"

"Certainly, Miss Ashperton."

"Oh, *do* tell me *all* about it." She sighed, fluttering her pale eyelashes at him over her nearsighted squint.

"I beg your pardon, miss, but I shouldn't wish to bore you with an account of libraries and museums. That's where I spend my time."

With that, her hero fell in ashes at her feet.

It was later in the evening when the company had assembled in Mrs. Ashperton's drawing room, newly redecorated in the latest Grecian style, that the hostess's carefully laid plans to snare a baronet for her daughter received another setback. Just as the tea tray was coming in, the noise of bustle in the foyer came to her ears. Then the alluring Lady Lurinda Ormsby swept into the room, as only the *Ne Plus Ultra* could sweep. "Dearest Aunt Lydia, forgive my unexpected arrival. I know I wasn't looked for until next week, but absolutely everyone has left London, and I couldn't abide it one moment longer."

She floated gracefully across the room to kiss Lady Ashperton, the light from the candelabra revealing the rich peacock blue of her dress against her peachy complexion and the auburn radiance of her hair. "Oh, dear, I see I am interrupting a party. I had no idea I would encounter one here in Yorkshire. Indeed, I had thought to escape the demands of sociability for a while. The London season has been exhausting. Oh, but, please, do be seated, gentlemen." She bestowed a universal smile on the men in the room who had all risen at her entrance.

The *Ne Plus Ultra* gracefully accepted a cup of tea from her aunt and looked around her, happy to be the center of attention in the crowded drawing room. "Why, Sir Brandley, do I dare to hope that you will remember me?" With a radiant smile she crossed to where Brandley stood.

"Of course, Lady Ormsby, and what an unexpected pleasure to see you again." Brandley bowed deeply. The Alluring Lurinda seated herself gracefully on the pale green silk sofa, allowing all the men in the room to resume their seats.

"And you have come from Cambridge simply covered with honors." Lurinda managed to hold her smile even while taking a sip from her cup.

Following her lead, Brandley took a long, slow sip of his tea, eyeing her levelly across the top of his cup. He would like to know what game she was playing. Then a spark of amusement kindled, and he settled into the cushions of the sofa. "I fear you must have found our mild Cambridge amusements rather dull after the glitter of a London season, Lady Ormsby."

"It had its moments of interest, Sir Brandley. But you really must call me Lurinda." She turned the full force of her charm on him.

"With pleasure, Lurinda. Might I add I have often heard you referred to as the Alluring Lurinda."

"Pray, sir, you shall put me to the blush."

"I find it impossible to believe that you are not thoroughly accustomed to receiving such compliments." He hoped the smile that he simply couldn't repress would be interpreted as a further compliment to her beauty. Brandley had never before found amusement in his disability, but to allow the *Ne Plus Ultra* to throw herself at his head and then see her confusion when she learned the truth was irresistible.

"Certainly, sir. But one becomes weary of the meaningless pleasantries of the ton. To receive a compliment from one with *your* intellectual faculties is a triumph indeed. You are the first man of letters of my acquaintance, Sir Brandley."

He bowed slightly. So he was a novelty.

Well, it was time. "Your tea has grown cold, Lurinda. May I bring you some more?"

The lady agreed. Brandley, for the first time in his life, took secret pleasure in limping slowly across a crowded drawing room.

But his plan went awry. When he returned to present the steaming cup, her eyes were shining. "Why, Sir Brandley, I had no idea — just like Lord Byron!"

Brandley almost choked on his mouthful of tea. She had put him in the same category with the clubfooted romantic poet who would stand in a brooding brown study at one side of a London assembly room while the ladies of the ton lionized him.

"I fear you mistake, My Lady. Whatever other unique qualifications I may possess, I am not a poet."

10

The next morning was wet and chill. Brandley settled himself comfortably in the library where he had directed that a small fire be laid in the fireplace. This was his favorite room at Okeford, with its dark woods, Persian rugs, and shelves of books reaching up to the high ceiling. Sometimes he worked at the massive carved mahogany desk in front of the windows, but today he chose a moroccan leather winged chair and a book on Caligula.

He had read less than ten pages, however, when Page started barking excitedly. "That's enough, Page." But the spaniel's deep bark continued. With an exasperated sigh, Brandley went to the door. Charlie and his corgis descended from a curricle in the pouring rain, surrounded by Brandley's hunting spaniels, each trying to outbark the others. Not waiting to get his hat and coat, Brandley hurried out to welcome his guest.

"Verdun, it's great to see you. I'm glad you accepted my invitation. Leave your luggage here. Reeth will bring it in." Charlie complied, but he was careful to bring his Manton's New Patent Shot Rifle in out of the rain. Brandley added more wood to the fire, and they dried off in the library.

"How long can you stay with us? Denton and I are having some excellent shooting."

"What I came for. My ramshackle cousin's such a bad shot he scared all the game away before I could aim at it. Fancies himself in the Byronic mold. Concentrating on game spoils his heroic pose."

"Oh, no. A brooding gudgeon with wild black hair, an open shirt collar, and a belcher tie?"

"And a dark soul. How the devil did you meet my cousin?"

"Know the type. Been cast for the role myself."

Charlie stared, speechless. "No, you're bamming me."

"Wish I were. But never mind. You'd best lay up here a few days. This shower won't last long; we can hunt tomorrow."

Early the next morning, they packed their rifles and a large hamper of food into the gig, collected the dogs, and set off through the mist, with the gamekeeper riding behind. Both young men wore nankeen breeches and black beaver hats. Charlie, however, had thrown on an old tweed coat, which he wore open over a high waistcoat. Croydon had sent Brandley out in a fitted hunting coat of dark green.

The covert was in a little valley with a swollen stream rushing through the grove of tall oaks. Soon the dogs picked up a scent. On the first flush, each man shot a pheasant, which fell in bracken at the end of the field, requiring skillful retrieves by the dogs through stiff cover.

The hunters moved farther into the field as Whipper roused three pigeons. With quick reflexes, Brandley shot one straight overhead, and it almost landed on top of them. Whipper ran to retrieve it, not three feet from his master's boot. Brandley let the dog work. "Good boy, Whipper. Find us some more." Several birds fell well out and required long-distance retrieves by the spaniels, which Brandley controlled with the whistle he wore round his neck. The gamekeeper followed behind with the pony carrying the game bags.

At midday they returned to the hamper in the gig and ate by the brook, sharing thick slabs of cold meat and cheese with the spaniels.

After lunch they shot several hares. The gamekeeper expertly clasped the legs of their trophies in braces and hung the game over a branch he had trimmed for the purpose.

"This will keep Mrs. Wiggin happily mak-

151

ing meat pies for a week." Brandley surveyed their five full braces.

"Best sport I've had in ages. Hunting with that trigger-happy cousin of mine put me so off my shot I wasn't sure I'd recover my aim."

It was on the ride home that Charlie innocently destroyed the harmony of the day for Brandley. "Nearly forgot. Saw Widkham in London just before I left for York. Sends greetings."

"And how is our noble friend amusing himself this summer? Bored stiff until the London season starts, I daresay."

"Preparing to escort his grandmother to Bath when I saw him. She got a maggot in her head that nothing would do but to take the waters. Keep him occupied while the Silberts tramp around ruined castles."

As Brandley made no comment to this, Charlie continued, "Not for me to say, but I'd wager he means to offer for Elinor when she returns. Fine-looking couple they make, but he must be besotted to offer for a girl with no fortune. Rather thought he'd go for a London heiress. Of course, he has enough blunt for both of them; and I daresay he's fond enough of her to take her in her shift." Charlie failed to notice the grim look on Brandley's face.

"But will she like that kind of life? All the ado and social whirl? I thought she had more sense than that."

Charlie shrugged. "Never seen a girl who could resist a handsome, titled husband and life of social position and ease. What sapskull would suppose she would want to try?" The gig lurched at a rut in the road, and Brandley mechanically guided the horse. "Besides, a marquess is right below a duke. She probably took a notion into her head she'd fancy being a marchioness."

Although he could think of nothing less attractive than a life ruled by the social whims of the hour, Brandley had to admit that it might appeal to a high-spirited girl like Elinor. She would be a lovely adornment to Jack's life. But would he cherish her as she deserved? He reproached himself for the heavy oppression he felt in his chest. He should have known. Indeed, he did know. It had been obvious in so many ways, and yet . . . well, he guessed Pope had said it best — hope did spring eternal. *That's just fine,* he thought bitterly. *If this is the way it ends, one would be better off not to have one's hopes roused.*

When the hunters arrived back at Okeford, they found a carriage with a pair of high-stepping matched grays waiting at the door. "Devilishly fine horseflesh," Charlie said. "Looks like a London rig."

"Gwyneth must have callers," Brandley commented without interest.

A footman met the gentlemen with a message that Lady Calvert wanted them to join her in the drawing room.

"Not in our hunting clothes," Brandley replied. "You may tell Her Ladyship we will join her presently."

A summons to the drawing room in his present frame of mind did nothing to elevate Brandley's spirits. Sometime later when the baronet made his entrance, it was with a stormy countenance.

"I'm so glad you have returned, Brandley. Lady Ormsby has come in search of reading material, and I knew you would be the one to guide her." A little smile played at the corners of Gwyneth's mouth as Brandley made a rather stiff bow to the ladies.

"I should be much obliged, Sir Brandley. I thoughtlessly removed from London with very few of my books, and I find the Harrogate library sadly lacking in anything of real intellectual worth."

"I take it, then, that you seek something of an improving nature?" Brandley allowed her obvious ploy to lighten his dark mood.

"Most assuredly, sir. I find Mrs. Radcliffe

and those of her sort to be so, er, frivolous. Not really worth one's time."

"I have no doubt that the Okeford library can offer you something above that. Perhaps a volume or two of sermons?" He made a sweeping bow that indicated she should accompany him to the library. Charlie, who had appeared in the drawing room a few minutes before Brandley and had been staring moonstruck at the *Ne Plus Ultra* ever since, followed along.

Unable to resist a touch of irony, Brandley searched the shelves for a moment and then presented Lurinda with two leather-bound volumes. "Knowing your fondness for Lord Byron, I fancy you may find these to your liking."

She took the volumes and looked at them quizzically.

"In Rousseau's *New Eloisa*, I believe you may find philosophies similar to Byron's *Childe Harold's Pilgrimage*." Brandley indicated the green suede volume.

The lady's reply was a soft, "Oh?" and a raised eyebrow.

"And Byron was strongly influenced in his composition of *Don Juan* by Volney's *The Ruins of Empires*."

"Oh?" the lady replied on a louder note and raised the other eyebrow. "I *do* thank you. I'm sure I shall find these most instructive."

"I am happy to have been of service. And now for the sermons . . ." Brandley returned to the shelves, but the lady hastily assured him the volumes she held would be adequate. Brandley escorted her to her waiting carriage.

A few days later, Charlie left Okeford. Brandley continued his reading, his visits with Dr. Midgeholme, and his hunting with Denton; but now the activities failed to raise his spirits as they had at first — even though punctuated with occasional amusing encounters with the *Ne Plus Ultra*. Memories of the joy he had known just a few weeks before haunted him. He tried to rationalize the scene in the Silberts' garden. Naturally Elinor was effervescent — it was her first day at home since the accident. Naturally Jack was attentive — it had happened on his estate. Naturally the scene looked intimate — well, how *could* he explain that?

Another week dragged by. Thursday morning Brandley refused Calvert's invitation to accompany him into Harrogate, deciding instead to try his hunters in a new covert. So Denton was alone that afternoon when he came out of his solicitor's office and suddenly found a small golden dog yapping insistently at his boots. Calvert looked around for the owner and spotted a young woman being handed out of a traveling chaise by an older man who looked vaguely familiar.

The father and daughter hurried forward to rescue the six-foot-man held at bay by the small animal. When the older man removed his hat and revealed a shining bald pate, memory clicked for Lord Calvert.

"Dr. Silbert, isn't it? What brings you so far afield from Cambridge?"

The professor would have launched into an explanation of his research undertakings in the middle of High Street had not Elinor interrupted. "Please accept my apologies for Mustard's behavior."

"Yes," seconded her father. "Oh, I'm sorry. Lord Calvert, this is my daughter Elinor."

"Delighted to meet you."

"I'd like you to meet Mrs. Silbert also. Won't you step to the chaise?"

Denton was hard put to hide his astonished amusement over the inaccuracy of his wife's deductions, which, he had to admit, he had abetted. "You must on no account break your journey here. The George is a most uncomfortable inn, and my wife would never forgive me if I didn't bring her brother's friends to Okeford."

Mrs. Silbert started to protest, but Denton capped his arguments. "You really have no notion of how happy Lady Calvert will be to receive you."

All the way back to Okeford a small smile played around Denton's mouth. He would teach Gwyneth a lesson for her overwrought conjectures.

Events fell in line without his maneuvering. Mustard needed a run in the garden, so Denton offered to send a footman to escort Miss Silbert in at her pleasure. "Make no hurry over it, my dear. We are quite at our leisure at Okeford."

Lady Calvert put down her needlework and rose as Lord Calvert ushered the Silberts into the blue salon. "My dear, I have unexpected happy news for you." His smile broadened. "I know you shall be astonished when I tell you that I encountered Dr. and Mrs. Silbert of Cambridge in Harrogate and have invited them to be our guests."

Gwyneth's eyes widened, but apart from that, she appeared to have been turned to stone. Calvert strode nearer his wife, took her motionless hand and extended it to Dr. Silbert, who bowed over the limp, lifeless member with composure.

"And Mrs. Silbert." Calvert directed his wife.

"Mrs. Silbert." Gwyneth's level voice betrayed no more emotion than her wooden body.

"I told the Silberts how deeply you regretted lack of opportunity to meet them in Cambridge. Happily, Dr. Silbert's studies have brought them north, so I insisted they stay with us. I knew how happy your brother would be to see his old friends. Perhaps you would like to instruct Mrs. Wiggin as to the rooms, my dear. I thought perhaps the rose room next to your brother's for Mrs. Silbert and the Chinese room in the north wing for Dr. Silbert?"

How Gwyneth would have replied to her husband's audacity would never be known, for at that moment the underfootman entered to announce Miss Silbert. Gwyneth's face came to life, and she swept across the room to greet Elinor.

Later when the Silberts had been escorted to their rooms to refresh themselves, Lady Calvert turned on her husband.

"You, sir, are the greatest rascal unhung! That you could have had the effrontery . . . that you could have let me believe . . . It is really the shabbiest behavior imaginable."

"It seems I mistook the matter." Except

for the mischievous twinkle in his eye, Denton was all contrition. "Pray forgive me. I was convinced you would be very happy to meet Miss Elinor Silbert."

"Gammon! Do you deny the whole scene was contrived to — to bum squabble me? You knew what I thought."

"I certainly did. Let that be a lesson to you the next time you are tempted to jump to conclusions. But own up, wasn't the relief worth the distress?"

Gwyneth burst into peals of laughter. Just before the Silberts joined them, however, she put her hand on Denton's arm. "Be warned, sir. I shall have a bit of my own back. Just you wait." Then she turned sharply as the Silberts entered. "My dear Mrs. Silbert, may I offer you some refreshment?"

The men immediately launched into a conversation, but Gwyneth noticed that Elinor seemed restless.

"Have you had a long journey today? Would you care to walk in the garden, Miss Silbert?"

"Only from Knaresborough, Lady Calvert. But I did leave my dog in the garden. Perhaps I should see that she is behaving herself, thank you. Will you excuse me, Mama?"

"Certainly, dear."

As Elinor left the room, she smiled to herself when she heard her father telling an attentive Lord Calvert about Geoffrey Chaucer's tribute to the duchess after she died of the plague. *Dearest Daddy does have a focused mind.*

Elinor had repressed the impulse to ask where Brandley was. She knew nothing of his aborted visit on his last evening in Cambridge, but she had been puzzled when her father later told her simply that Brandley had called to say farewell. She was disappointed too. She had chosen to wear her jonquil dress that day in anticipation of seeing him.

She was strolling by rose beds bursting with bloom when she heard horse's hooves on the gravel of the circular lane in front of the manor. She hurried forward and then came to a sudden halt. The rider alighting from a horse was not the tall dark man she had expected, but rather a stunningly beautiful red-haired woman in a dark blue riding habit.

It was too late to retreat. Elinor held her ground as the woman approached. "How do you do? I've come to see Sir Brandley. Is he in the garden?"

Elinor was surprised by the woman's proprietary air, but answered with civility. "I believe he may be out riding, but he is expected soon. We have only arrived a short time ago ourselves."

"Why, I believe you must be Brandley's friend from Cambridge. He has spoken of you. Your father is a tutor or something, is he not?"

"I am Elinor Silbert. My father is Dr. Silbert, Master of Peterhouse," Elinor replied.

"I daresay, I thought it was something like that." Lurinda took a red leather-bound book from her reticule. "I had hoped to see Brandley to discuss this volume with him. He is most refreshing after the sort of person one meets in London and so romantic — so Byronic . . . an air of mystery about him, don't you think? Well, my dear, it was delightful to meet you, but I must be going. Since Lady Calvert is engaged, I shan't bother her. I'll just leave this for Sir Brandley with the butler. After all, we're such near neighbors. I'm sure to see him again soon." Without waiting for a reply, Lurinda swept across the expanse of green lawn to the front door.

After walking up and down the garden with agitated steps, Elinor slackened her pace and turned to Mustard. "Well, Musty, what did you think of that?"

Mustard made no answer, but curled her lips back to reveal her sharp little teeth. "Yes, that's precisely what I thought too."

A few moments later barking dogs announced their master's return from his afternoon ride. Brandley, his dogs at his heels, approached the garden from the stables.

Elinor waited excitedly, remembering how often during the past month she had thought of seeing him again, of watching his face light in surprise, of seeing his grin, of sharing a smile of affectionate amusement as he called her Daphne or she accused him of being bacon-brained. She forced herself to stand still, holding her breath while her heart thumped in her throat. She heard two birds fluttering in the tree above her. A bee buzzed from flower to flower. And then came the sound she was waiting for — the gate in the hedge squeaked.

Brandley was looking down, talking to Whipper. As he looked up, the words died on his lips. Nothing in all her daydreams of this moment had prepared her for the hard, grim countenance she saw as he stood stockstill looking at her.

"Well, if that's the way Apollo treated Daphne, it's no wonder she preferred the life of a laurel tree." Elinor managed to hide her confusion behind a bright, if slightly forced,

163

smile. *He doesn't want to see me! What could have happened? He's never been rude before.* And then the unwelcome answer forced itself upon her — Lurinda.

Innate courtesy triumphed over wounded pride, and Brandley limped forward to bow and assure her of a welcome. But the excited barking of Brandley's dogs and Mustard's shrill yips made conversation impossible. Brandley commanded silence. Order returned to the rose garden as Whipper sniffed at the little intruder. The two dogs touched noses amicably and then made off together toward the stable — Whipper leading the way as Mustard trotted half a length behind.

Elinor, with some reserve, told Brandley about meeting Lord Calvert in the village. But his eyes remained unyielding as he escorted her back to the house, courteous and stiff.

Brandley greeted Dr. and Mrs. Silbert and then excused himself to change clothes. Elinor was hurt and puzzled. Their relationship had been so warm, so easy, so mutual in its shared delights.

A few minutes later, the entire party dispersed to dress for dinner. Gwyneth sent Burney to serve her guests. The efficient maid unpacked Elinor's things, smoothed the wrinkles from her ivory muslin gown with the pink ribbons, and was waiting to help her change and to arrange her hair. To Elinor, who had encountered a dresser only in books, this was a rare treat, though she thought it a bit silly to be dressed by a servant when she had been doing it herself since she had left the nursery. Hair-dressing was one of Burney's specialities, and Elinor's golden, curly locks were a delight to work with. Burney arranged the tresses with a center part, waving to tiny ringlets at each ear and a crown of curls on top.

"There, miss. You look lovely, just like a June evening." Burney placed a pink band of ribbon in front of the curls and admired her work with satisfaction.

"Thank you, Burney, but it's July." Elinor laughed, pleased with her own reflection in the mirror. She hoped Brandley would notice.

Just then there was a knock at the door. Burney opened it to admit Gwyneth and left to have Elinor's traveling dress ironed. Lady Calvert was radiant in a coral gown of light fabric with white silk flowers embroidered on the skirt and short full sleeves. A pale silk stole draped gracefully over her arms and fell to the floor. "I thought I'd see if you were ready and take you down to dinner myself." Gwyneth smiled at her lovely guest.

"You look charming, my dear. My brother is fortunate to have such special friends in Cambridge. I was disappointed that I didn't get to meet you when we were there."

Elinor was relieved. She had wondered if Brandley's aloofness might have sprung from family opposition to their friendship. Despite the Silberts' gentility, none of her family lines rose to the ranks of nobility. Elinor showed her relief in her voice. "Oh, thank you. We have enjoyed Brandley's company so much. Mama wouldn't know what to do without his help on her Grecian subjects, and Daddy is anxious to continue their discussions about some of the classical allusions in the *Book of the Duchess*."

Gwyneth's warm smile encouraged Elinor to continue. A pale blush stained her cheeks. "But he didn't seem very happy to see me. I wondered, perhaps . . . that is — is he well? I mean — when he rescued me from my fall in the woods . . . he didn't injure himself, did he? I'd never forgive myself." After meeting Lurinda, this wasn't the question uppermost in Elinor's mind, but she was struggling to find reasons for the rift other than the obvious one, which she didn't want to consider at all.

"No, he's fine. The strongest he's ever been. But what are you talking about?"

Gwyneth's wide eyes and furrowed brow mirrored the intensity of her interest.

"Then he didn't tell you?"

Gwyneth shook her head, so Elinor told her of the turned ankle and Brandley's carrying her back to the house. Gwyneth's eyes were misty when Elinor finished.

"Yes, that's just what he would do. He never did lack for courage." She spoke quietly.

"No," said Elinor slowly. "Not in that way. . . ."

"You've seen that too?" Gwyneth's voice softened almost to a whisper. "You're very perceptive, my dear. But the courage to overcome self-doubt is not something most of us have such deep need of. And I'm not sure it's something that can be found alone. A sister is most inadequate." The last sentence was spoken thoughtfully as if after careful decision that Elinor was indeed the right person to hear her thoughts.

"Yes, I'm sure that's right." Elinor nodded. "That's why it hurts so when he shuts me out." Gwyneth smiled as she took Elinor's hand and led her from the bedroom.

They walked past several doors down a long, wide hallway to the gallery above the broad, curving oak stairway. Elinor could imagine musicians playing in the gallery while guests gathered in the reception room below for a ball. She had attended many such events in the pages of books. At the foot of the staircase, they turned to the left to enter a small sitting room where the others were gathered. The company was engaged in a lively discussion of whose treachery was worse — Anetor, who betrayed Troy, or Ganelon, who procured the betrayal of Roland. "I told you Daddy missed Brandley," Elinor whispered to Gwyneth in a conspiratorial tone, light rushing into her eyes as she looked at him.

Dr. Silbert looked up as the women entered, and Brandley's glance followed. The vision of Elinor framed in the doorway, candlelight burnishing her hair, smiling softly at him, made him break off in midsentence. This time he didn't stand rooted as he had in the garden, but he came to her just behind her father, who crossed the room exclaiming, "Ah, there's my princess."

Calvert offered his arm to escort Mrs. Silbert in to dinner, and Dr. Silbert requested that his hostess do him the honor. As Brandley smiled at Elinor, the light from the fireplace struck the planes of his face and highlighted the strength of his features. Elinor accepted his arm.

The wainscotted room with its pale silk

wall coverings and crimson damask uphol-
stery held none of the stiff formalism Elinor
expected in a great house. It was alive and
inviting with glowing candlelight and delec-
table aromas. Their discussion, which
ranged from ancient Roman mythology to
contemporary Parliamentary debates, began
with the soup and took them through the
second course of partridges, accompanied by
broiled mushrooms and French beans, with
dressed crab and artichoke bottoms in sauce.
Even Brandley approached his food with unusual appetite. And Elinor, careful to absorb
every detail, felt something like a tiny shock
every time Brandley smiled at her across the
table.

Footmen removed the dishes, and the
guests helped themselves to sweets and nuts
from silver bowls. Then the women retired
to the library, leaving the men to their
brandy and political talk unfit for feminine
ears.

On a low table by one of the chairs Elinor
caught sight of a slim red book she had seen
earlier that day. She moved to the other side
of the room and tried to ignore it. But it was
impossible to escape the irrational feeling
that the book was laughing at her. Finally,
she gathered her courage and met the subject head-on. "Oh, Lady Calvert, I met your

neighbor while I was in the garden today."

"My neighbor? Whom do you mean?"

"She didn't actually introduce herself, but she said she was a neighbor and that she had called to return a book your brother had loaned her."

"Oh, I see." Gwyneth laughed. "I didn't know we had been honored with a visit from Lady Ormsby. The Alluring Lurinda, Calvert calls her, but her official title, bestowed by the *haut ton* is *Ne Plus Ultra*. The North Riding has been considerably exercised to discover why we should have been honored by so extended a visit from one of London's luminaries. But a letter I received this morning from a friend in London has shed some light on that. The on dit there is that she fled London rather than face the embarrassment of her failure to bring the Marquis d'Eliante up to scratch when he returned to Paris without having offered for her."

Elinor was unsure whether she should take comfort or alarm, but she had little time to consider the matter because the gentlemen soon joined them. Calvert produced two chessboards. Brandley challenged Professor Silbert on a Chinese board of carved green and white jade. Calvert's white queen attacked Elinor's forces on a board of alternating silver and gold squares.

170

In the easy return to old times, Brandley visibly thawed. Elinor felt the last bastion had been stormed when Mustard curled herself at his feet and Page didn't utter the slightest protest.

Elinor had no idea what had caused the strange reception she had received, but the fact that all appeared well now was enough for her at the moment. It seemed that it had to be when dealing with such a sensitive temperament as Brandley's. The fact that she was willing to put up with it all showed her, if she had needed any evidence, the depth of her caring.

But lifting her chin firmly with a toss of her head, she determined that whatever the cause of Brandley's bad mood, she would do everything possible to prevent it happening again in the future.

11

Calvert had suggested an outing to the ruins of Fountains Abbey, which Mrs. Silbert would sketch and the rest of the company would simply enjoy. His guests agreed, and so the following day found the party riding along the shaded country lanes toward Ripon with Page and Mustard capering at the horses' heels. After riding for a while with her mother and Gwyneth, Elinor pulled aside to ride with Brandley.

The lane wound through thick woodland, and golden patches of sun fell between deep shadows, making a striking chiaroscuro like a Rembrandt painting.

Elinor gazed in every direction, taking in its beauty. "I do wish we'd see a deer." She spoke quietly, as if fearful of frightening one that might be just around the corner.

"Let's keep a lookout. It's not impossible, although evening is a better time. They come to the streams to drink then."

The horses moved rhythmically, and Elinor smiled at the world around her.

"I almost forgot to tell you — before going to Bolingbroke, we spent a week with my sister Joan." She turned slightly in her side-saddle to face him more directly.

"Joan?" He frowned briefly. "I'd nearly forgotten you had a sister. Didn't you tell me she's married to a vicar?"

"Yes. The Reverend Michael Cowles. He has the living at Chatteris. We've never been close. She was married when I was still in the schoolroom, and I see her so seldom; but this time she seemed so different." Elinor's mount flicked her ears forward and tossed her head as a rabbit ran across the road in front of them. Elinor reached forward and patted the horse's neck.

"Well, I suppose people do change as they get older."

"No, it wasn't just that. I always thought Joan was awfully restless. And she never seemed to be really happy either. But this time she was so . . . so at peace with herself." Elinor paused to consider her own words. "Yes, that's it — peace. That's what was lacking before. Always complaining that dispensing her little charities and meeting with the ladies' benevolent society just weren't enough to spend a life on."

"But this time?" Brandley's question showed his interest. He had been wrestling with his own lack of satisfaction.

"That's what I wanted to tell you about. You've heard of Robert Hall?"

Brandley nodded. Everyone had heard of the greatest nonconformist preacher in England. "Isn't he the one whose sermon on the death of Princess Charlotte was quoted in all the papers?" England had been stunned by the death, in childbirth, of their beautiful crown princess and her baby. Brandley was only fourteen at the time. "Don't know much about him, but I couldn't forget the sermon. Dr. Midgeholme read me long passages from the *Morning Post* in awed tones. 'That masterpiece — delivered at half an hour's notice — half an hour!'" Brandley stabbed the air with a finger in imitation of his old tutor. "'And without notes! Inspired genius, my boy, that's what it is!'"

"Well, your Dr. Midgeholme must have been right," Elinor said chuckling. "Hall preached in my brother-in-law's parish this spring. Not in the church, of course, but in a Baptist chapel in the village. My sister and her husband wouldn't have dreamed of going to hear a dissenter. But her very good friend went. The next morning Mary interrupted Joan at the breakfast table to tell her about it. You can imagine how shocked Joan was, not only that her friend would go to such a meeting, but that she should be so enthusiastic. It seems Hall had preached a remarkable sermon — about true religion being consistent with a love of freedom — and about discovering it in a personal way."

For Brandley, to whom Mount Olympus and its inhabitants were more real than any heavenly beings, this sounded absurd. "Most certainly I know all about personal relationships with gods." He thought of the legends in which Zeus had taken various forms to seduce beautiful mortal maidens. "Danae and the shower of gold, Leda and the swan, Europa and the bull. Don't tell me *that's* the source of your sister's happiness!" He finished with light irreverence, his eyes bright with laughter.

Elinor immediately caught the absurdity of Zeus in the form of a white bull abducting her very proper sister. She smiled.

"Oh, Brandley, if you knew my sister . . . But it's really most amazing. She did go with Mary the next night. And she was actually excited about Hall — his force and magnetism. Anyway, she says it's *true*. She really has found God in a personal way."

"I must say, that's some story. What do you make of it?" His eyes narrowed skeptically.

"I don't know, but she's happier than I've

ever known her to be, and she was certainly more fun to visit than before." Elinor shrugged.

"What does your brother-in-law have to say to all this?"

"Of course, Michael's skeptical of anything that smacks of nonconformity, but he can't help but enjoy having a happy wife. There is something about her. I don't know . . ."

The pause grew longer and longer as each was engrossed in private thoughts. The sound of their horses' hooves striking the hard dirt sounded distant.

Finally Brandley broke the silence. "You should meet Nurse. I don't know if she claims any special relationship with its Author, but she sure relates to the Good Book. She has a store of Scriptural quotations for any situation." Brandley smiled at old memories. "You should have heard her take after Calvert when he and Gwyneth became attached. He had been something of a rake in his day. Nurse didn't approve, and she really opened up her store for him. Said that his end would be a lesson to sinners and that the increase of his fields would be given to the caterpillar."

By now they were approaching the abbey. The path wound through a fine old park under huge oaks. There was little under-brush, and wildflowers grew in patches of sunlight.

"The abbey was founded in 1132 by Cistercian monks from York." Calvert's explanation to Professor Silbert floated back to the couple.

Brandley was increasingly aware of Elinor's closeness as they rode side by side, absorbing the peace of the placid stream running beside the flowered path. He longed to reach out and take her hand as her mount stayed companionably close to Emrys.

Suddenly Elinor pulled her horse up. "Oh, it's lovely!"

The others followed her pointing arm to the view of the great abbey's square tower framed by forest and fronted by still water and deep grass.

It was yet some distance away. As they approached by the winding path, the building disappeared now and again, only to reveal itself from some new viewpoint a moment later. But Brandley was more intent on viewing the raptures reflected in Elinor's face. In spite of any understanding she might have with Lord Widkham, he wanted to speak — to let her know what was in his heart.

"Elinor," he began softly.

But at that moment the party rode down the last little hillock and arrived at the ancient landmark. Gwyneth exclaimed over the glories of its Gothic architecture and the lush edging of green grass growing along the top of all the roofless walls. Mrs. Silbert was struck by the contrasting combination of yew and chestnut trees.

"Seven of the enormous yew trees are said to be 1,400 years old," Calvert informed her.

"I can almost see the monks in their habits walking in the fields and woods and hear the convent bell and the chanting of the hours," Elinor mused.

But Brandley said nothing. He silently sorted and stored his new memories. Elinor would soon be gone, and he would need them.

Before further exploring the abbey, they rode over to the little village of Studley and ate a cold luncheon at the White Hart. The host set the table in his best parlor with a white cloth, pewter plates, and a bowl of the daisies that bloomed in profusion just outside the leaded casements of the rustic room. It was not usual at his remote inn to serve people of quality, and thoughts of his bill assured his broad smile and attentive service.

When they returned to the abbey, Mrs. Silbert continued her sketching, and her husband chose to keep her company. The others went for a leisurely stroll through the field of daisies. After a while they sat in the shade of a tree by a stream. Even Mustard and Page were happy for a rest, but Elinor gathered an armful of wildflowers. Brandley considered joining her, then thought better of it. Stooping was so hard for him. But he enjoyed watching. He helped her weave the daisies into chains with which she bedecked all of their party, including Mustard.

Gwyneth, with a knowing smile, requested Calvert to accompany her back to the abbey, leaving the couple to themselves.

Elinor leaned contentedly against the trunk of the shading tree, and Brandley, reclining near her, played idly with a clump of meadow grass. He pulled a blade slowly through his fingers — noting the sharpness of the edges, the smoothness on one side, and the slight fuzziness on the other.

"This puts me in mind of lines I learned in the schoolroom," Elinor mused dreamily. " 'The secluded scene impresses thoughts of more deep seclusion and connects the landscape with the quiet of the sky. The day is come when I again repose here under this dark sycamore —' It's a chestnut, isn't it? Miss Trilling would be shocked by my paraphrase. *Tintern Abbey* was her favorite

Wordsworth. She made us memorize the whole thing."

Brandley paused, his fingers poised midway along another blade of grass. *"And this green pastoral landscape were to me more dear for themselves and for thy sake!"* His mind finished the poem, but it wouldn't do to say that to another man's intended. "Who was Miss Trilling?" Much safer ground.

"My governess. Papa was shockingly progressive in his notions about educating females. He said he didn't want his daughter turned into a bluestocking, but he did want to be able to talk to me. So he turned the upstairs parlor into a classroom, and Miss Trilling taught the two boys of the vicar of St. Mary's and a son and daughter of a professor friend of Papa's as well."

Brandley plucked a blade of grass and twirled it between his fingers. He was quiet, hoping she'd go on. She did. Her eyes were soft and her look faraway as she smiled at memories of her happy childhood.

"Mornings were for the classroom — history, mathematics, literature. Afternoons were best. She led us on expeditions to study architecture, horticulture, history."

Brandley knew Elinor's memories were filled with happiness and friendships. He tried to push back his own. When he allowed

180

himself to think about it, his early childhood seemed a blur of hushed voices, efficient hands, darkened rooms. Then the hands and voices went away and left only the relentless pain. Then the pain receded and left a wallow of weakness and the ignominy of having to be carried about, the humiliation of strength that failed again and again. Once it was almost conquered, he could sit up and look about, perhaps in the garden if it was a fine day; then off to London again to be examined by yet another surgeon, and the process began anew. With each surgery he could only hope to faint before the pain became really unbearable and he had to suffer the added disgrace of crying. If he just wouldn't come around again before it was over . . . He sometimes wondered whether it was the disease itself that had left him maimed or the treatment of the physicians.

He tore at the blade of grass. Elinor was telling about a birthday party, and he thought of Gwyneth's attempts to provide companions for him. The first had ended abruptly when the adults left the room, and his three active guests tumbled outside to play leapfrog on the lawn, leaving him lonely and chafing at his lameness. The second had been worse. Gwyneth had cautiously invited only one child, Mrs. Ashperton's nephew

Andrew. The snakes-and-ladders board game held the guest's attention until the supply of sweetmeats gave out. Andrew then impatiently swept the figures from the board. "You're no fun. I want to go home." Andrew's embarrassed aunt bore him home in disgrace. Mercifully, Gwyneth had not tried again. Brandley threw away the mutilated grass.

It was time to return. The ride back to Okeford was pleasant but quieter. The pull of old memories stayed with Brandley and, in the near silence of the ride, played tricks with his mind. The firm, steady rhythm of Emrys's stride became his own, and Brandley pictured himself covering the ground with long, forceful strides. And then as the path led through the green hollow of a gentle dale, he saw himself breaking into a strong, swift run that skimmed the earth easily without a halt or a stumble, without tiredness or pain.

That was what Elinor deserved in a man, no doubt what she herself wanted. A cripple could be a pleasant enough companion for an afternoon outing, but no more.

Leaving the path, Brandley kicked Emrys to a gallop across a field that offered the distraction of stone walls to be jumped. His mind went back to the myths on which he wrote his book. Bellerphon had been punished for presumption in trying to ride Pegasus and condemned to go through life maimed and alone. Was this to be his punishment also? Were the clouds meting out vengeance on him for presuming to look too high? Was his penalty not the physical pain he had already suffered, but the emotional torment of being forever cut off from the joy of Elinor's companionship? If only he had never met her. All he could do now was guard himself against such moments of vulnerability as this afternoon.

It seemed Brandley's resolution was to be easily kept. Shortly after dinner, the Silberts requested their host and hostess to excuse them. They would like to retire early as they would be continuing their journey the next morning. Calvert had tried to persuade the professor to remain another day for some shooting, but he was not to be deterred.

So after arranging that the next morning he himself would escort their party across March Ghyll Moor where Cobbett could then easily pick up the old Roman road en route to Clitheroe, Calvert bowed his guests from the parlor.

"Will you be going by way of Bolton Priory, love?" Gwyneth's question was casual, but she seemed to listen carefully for Denton's affirmative answer. Then she stood quickly and crossed the room. "Why is Mrs. Wiggin so slow in sending up the tea tray? I shall go ask her to have it served in the library." Gwyneth swept from the room, apparently forgetting that she could simply have rung.

Not many minutes later she joined her brother and husband in the library, sat gracefully at the Queen Anne table, and with only a tiny smile to indicate that her mind was not wholly on the activity at hand, began pouring out from the ornate silver pot.

Denton offered a few casual remarks about the day's outing, but Brandley wanted to steer the conversation away from anything personal. He recounted Elinor's story of her sister's religious experience. Rather to his surprise, Calvert did not laugh.

Returning his teacup to his wife for a refill, the viscount nodded thoughtfully. "Yes, I've heard such stories before. Puts me in mind of my boyhood. One of my grandfather's favorite reminiscences was of attending one of the Countess of Huntingdon's salons when George Whitefield preached there. She was famous for bullying her fashionable friends to her drawing room to be converted. Lord Chesterfield and the Earl of Boling-broke were there when my grandfather attended." He took a long sip of tea.

Gwyneth was now fully intent on the conversation. "What an intriguing story. What did they think of such a thing?"

"It obviously made a great impression on my grandfather, as he told the story often. It seems neither Chesterfield nor Bolingbroke was converted, but both thought Whitefield a truly remarkable man. The Duchess of Buckingham, on the other hand, found it all highly offensive and insulting — the idea of the members of the peerage having sins that needed to be forgiven!"

"Whatever became of the Countess of Huntingdon?"

"Devoted her life and fortune to Methodism, it seems. She built chapels, helped the poor — saw that they were fed physically as well as spiritually — which I must say makes a great deal of sense." He gave his empty cup to his wife, but after she refilled it, he decided he didn't want more.

"She must have quite sunk herself socially."

"With the Duchess of Buckingham, at least. But it was said that George III admired her greatly. Of course, he was pious enough himself. But even Edmund Burke encouraged her fight against atheism."

"Well, against *atheism*, of course,"

Gwyneth agreed readily. Her churchgoing habits were regular enough, and as a member of the nobility, she always did her duty to set the proper example for the lower orders. "But all of this Wesleyan zeal and in the upper classes even, becoming fanatic about religion — it's too much."

Brandley thought so too, but his scholarly habits had trained him to remain open-minded to intellectual inquiry. He would like to hear more.

Later, however, alone in his room, Brandley's thoughts soon left theology to wander back through the hours of the day. His newly erected bulwarks against vulnerability crumbled to dust as he relived the moments of laughing with Elinor, exploring the abbey with Elinor, strolling through a field of daisies with Elinor. He uttered an oath and threw his book on the bed. Why couldn't she have stayed in Cambridge and married her marquess? Why did she have to come all the way up here and disturb his peace? Peace? What peace? Well, all right, he hadn't been at peace, but this gnawing pain inside — that hadn't been there before.

It was early the next morning before he fell into a restless sleep, so he was in none too good a humor when he went down to breakfast. He hoped the others would have already eaten. The Silberts planned to go on to Skipton today en route to Clitheroe Castle. As this was an easy ride, especially since Denton was taking them in a shortcut across the moor, they did not plan an early start. Brandley's hope for solitude was not to be granted him. Elinor was just accepting a second cup of coffee from a footman when Brandley entered the room.

"Good morning, Brandley. I've just been thinking what a delightful visit we've had here. I hate to go on so soon. I hoped Lord Calvert would be able to entice Papa to stay longer with the promise of a hunting party, but Papa is in such a hurry to get on to Clitheroe and Lancaster. I have enjoyed getting to know your sister. I promised Amy and Peter I would take them on a walk in the garden after breakfast. Won't you join us?" Elinor paused for breath. "Oh, I've run on like a fiddlestick! But you look positively bleak. Aren't you even going to wish me good morning?"

Her radiance was irresistible. So, telling himself she would be gone in a short time anyway, Brandley quickly finished his coffee and accompanied Elinor and the children into the yard.

Amy was all smiles and took off immediately chasing a butterfly, but Peter was in one of his moods. He kicked at a clod beside a flower bed. "Why can't I go to Clitheroe too? I want to see the castle. I could help the professor. I can climb anything."

Brandley shrugged. "Yes, you've certainly demonstrated that. But you know Dr. Midgeholme is coming over to give you a Latin lesson this morning. Matter of fact, you'd best be off to Nana for a wash-up before he gets here."

Peter gave a parting kick at the clod and turned away. Brandley tried to catch up with Elinor and Amy. Keeping up with a three-year old, however, could hardly be called a leisurely stroll. Brandley followed with dragging step as Elinor laughingly chased after the vivacious toddler while Mustard frolicked and barked around them. Fortunately, Nana soon came to claim her charge, and Elinor breathlessly joined Brandley.

"Let's sit in the arbor," she pleaded. "How could anything so small move so fast?"

When they entered the honeysuckle arbor, Elinor moved a book from a chair and sat down with a sigh.

"I don't remember leaving a book here." Brandley glanced at it.

"Oh, that's mine. I was reading here before breakfast. Good thing we found it, or

I'd have forgotten to take it with me."

He turned the volume over in his hand. *Buck on Richard III.* It was quite illogical that something so innocent should have brought his dark mood to the surface, but it did. "Just what is your fascination with deformities?" He lashed out at her, all the old bitterness surging up in him, drawing the lines deep in his face.

"What? Richard? But he wasn't. The hunchback was just a dramatic device. . . ." She broke off as the full realization of his meaning swept in upon her. Such an absurdity was simply too much for her patience, and her own rarely roused anger flared. "How can you be such — such an imbecile! You're not Apollo. You're Narcissus! You can't get your mind off yourself long enough to think of anyone else's feelings!" She hurled the words at him and ran to the house. Lurinda could have him and welcome.

12

An hour later Brandley glanced from his window to see the Silberts, Mustard, and their luggage packed in the carriage being driven from the yard by Cobbett following Calvert. Brandley turned from the window. He had put off Peter's requests to go fishing for several days, and the vicar's lesson should be at an end by now. It might be a good time to fulfill the postponed promise.

However, Peter was nowhere to be found. He had not reported for his washing-up, and Dr. Midgeholme had tired of waiting and left. Nana thoroughly searched the upstairs and downstairs nurseries. Reeth combed the stables, and three footmen covered the garden and front lawn. Gwyneth came to her brother in distress. "Where do you suppose he could have gone? He's not allowed to ride out alone — although he does sometimes sneak off — but his pony is in the stable. Nana thought he had gone to the stables with his father, but no one has seen him since before the Silberts left." She turned to the window wringing her hands.

The act of turning toward the window jogged Brandley's memory. He had noticed the lid to the luggage box on the back of the Silberts' chaise bouncing as if not tightly tied when they started down the drive, but he had thought no more of it. Now the size and shape of the box in relation to the size and shape of his nephew seemed strikingly coincidental. He thought he could almost recall seeing a little hand on the edge of the rim.

"I assure you, he's no more damaged than a few bruises, sister. It's odds to ounces Calvert has discovered him by now, but I'll ride after him to make sure."

The worried furrows remained on Gwyneth's brow.

"Don't be alarmed. The only harm he's likely to come to is a good hiding from his father." And then because she looked so genuinely distressed, Brandley gave her a reassuring kiss on the cheek. "Won't be above two hours, I promise. Unless those dark clouds provide some mischief." He glanced at the sky.

Nothing could surpass the moors for their wild beauty. Intent as he was on his errand, the remoteness and solitude of the green and rocky country reached Brandley. Even when he had to ride a considerable distance around a flock of sheep and the threatening rain clouds overcame the sun's last valiant efforts to provide warmth, the sense of wonder at the sweep of the desolate country remained with him.

A cold rain had been falling for some time before Brandley began to feel his frustration rising at having seen no sign of the travelers. His concern increased as he realized that if Peter was stowed away in the luggage box with its loose lid bouncing over every rut in the road, it would soon be as full of cold water as a fish pond. That aggravating child would be soaking for a case of ague. Not that it wouldn't serve him right.

Ducking his head against a fresh spurt of rain blown by a sharp wind, Brandley muttered an oath and turned Emrys toward a rise of ground. From that elevation he hoped he might be able to locate his quarry. "What is it, Page? You see something?" The spaniel had begun giving sharp little barks a short distance up the road. Brandley looked down the slope across the river toward Bolton Priory. "Well, I don't see anything, boy, but you may be right. Calvert said they'd go that way."

Brandley gave Emrys his head across the distance of moorland, jumped the river at a narrow spot, and then pulled up short. A dark shape on the road ahead could be the carriage he sought. But if so, why were they stopped dead still in the middle of the road?

A few paces closer Brandley saw the answer. Two surly highwaymen blocked the road, one with his pistol leveled straight at Denton, the other holding Cobbett and those inside the chaise. Brandley's worst fear was for the child. If Peter should spring up suddenly, the gunman might shoot first and then find out it was only a child.

Surprise was Brandley's only weapon. He slipped off his jacket and nudged Emrys off the road around the corner of the abbey's garden wall. When he surveyed the height of the wall, he realized the desperation of his plan. It was the highest jump he had ever asked of Emrys, and in the rain the horse couldn't be sure of a firm footing. But he could see no other way.

Giving Emrys a short run from which to spring, he kicked him into a gallop and leaned forward in the saddle. They flew over the wall, landing almost on top of the highwayman holding Calvert. At the same moment, Brandley gave a fierce yell and pitched his water-logged coat at the other gunman.

The plan would have worked perfectly except for two things. Cobbett had followed the gunman's orders to dismount, and the Silbert chaise was driverless. The spirited pair bolted, dragging the carriage down a lane awash with mud.

And as Brandley had feared, Emrys came down in a puddle with a slick clay bottom. The horse fought to gain his footing, but the rider, already somewhat off balance from flinging his coat at the gunman, was unable to steady him. Emrys floundered, and Brandley was flung off the left side into a pool of mire.

Wiping the filth from his eyes, Brandley sat up just in time to see the amazing sight of the highwayman throwing his gun away and galloping down the road to stop the bolting carriage with Cobbett pursuing on foot.

And then he saw Calvert pull the mask off his assailant, who had also abandoned his weapon and was blubbering, "Right sorry, I am, M'Lord. We didn't mean no 'arm. It were all a 'um."

"A hum!" Calvert obviously failed to see the humor. "Do you mean to tell me you accost people on open roads for a lark?"

"Not regular like, M'Lord."

"Wait a minute! How do you know I'm a lord?" Calvert grabbed the man by his lapels and pulled him closer, almost dragging him from his horse. "Don't I know you? Aren't you the man the gardener took on to help with the new plantings?"

The would-be criminal hung his head.

"Yes, M'Lord. Turrible sorry, M'Lord. But we wouldn't of 'urt nobody. She said ye'd be much diverted, said she promised to get a bit of her own back."

"Gwyneth!" Calvert remembered her threat to get even with him.

" 'Spect somethun went awry though. Didn't look to find no carriage with you — and that young man flyin' over the wall like a bat outta 'ell. Cooee, I never seed the like."

Calvert dropped the blubbering man at these words and spun around in his saddle. "Hilliard, is that you? What did you think you were doing? You could have been killed!" He looked down at his brother-in-law still sitting in the mud. "Are you planning to sit there for the rest of the afternoon?"

"The deuce of it is, I don't seem to be able to get up." Brandley said it as lightly as he could, but the situation was really beyond endurance. His heroic rescue was turned to a farce with the knowledge that the holdup was a charade.

"The carriage will be back in a moment. You can go —"

"No! Blast it! Get me on my horse."

Denton didn't argue, but led Emrys over to where Brandley was leaning on the under-gardener cum highwayman.

"Hurry!" Brandley ground at them, ignoring the pain in his lower back and hip. But the slosh of the carriage wheels told him that they were too late. He now had to suffer the final ignominy of having Elinor see him being hoisted onto his horse like a sack of potatoes. And now, at the moment when the rain would have served for a welcome screen and a shower to wash some of the mud off him, the sky cleared.

"If you care to look in the luggage box, you may find something of interest." Brandley turned Emrys sharply. As he rode away, he heard the carriage stop and Elinor call his name, but he didn't pause.

Anger was his greatest ally to keep him in the saddle in spite of wet, muddy clothes, humiliating thoughts, and physical pain. Fury at his sister who had been so caper-witted as to set up that scam; fury at his nephew whose cries even now reached him as he received a tongue-lashing from his father, which would be nothing compared to his later chastisement; but mostly fury at himself that in his one great chance to appear heroic before Elinor, he had failed miserably.

By the time Calvert arrived at Okeford with Peter and the doctor had been summoned, however, Brandley's fury at Peter had changed to deep concern. After a cursory examination, the doctor scolded Brandley for his neck-or-nothing riding and assured him he'd be uncomfortable for a few days. "But not less than you deserve. I'd tell you to take it easy and give yourself a chance if I thought I'd be heeded." He was far less complacent, though, about the child.

"Keep him wrapped in blankets, hot bricks at his feet." The doctor barked his orders to Gwyneth and Nana. "All the barley water he can drink and, if he seems feverish, a saline draught. No hot wine or any of your old wives' cures."

Gwyneth squared her shoulders. "Certainly not, doctor. I am not a stranger to the sickroom and am accounted by many to be a tolerable nurse."

The doctor glanced at Brandley who had received her nursing in the past. "Yes, so I recall. Very well. I gave him some laudanum so he will sleep, but do not leave him alone. I expect fever and much restlessness. Keep him covered and give him all the fluids he'll take. I'll be back tomorrow morning."

There was no question but that Gwyneth would take the first round of nursing. Nana returned to Amy in the upstairs nursery, and Brandley and Calvert each went to their rooms. Well after midnight Brandley wakened and decided he was not likely to sleep again. He made his way to Peter's room. Gwyneth was sitting quietly in an armchair by the bedside, a screen between the bed and her small table to shield Peter from the light of the lamp. "How is he?"

Gwyneth looked terribly tired, but she managed a small smile for her brother. "He's sleeping well due to the laudanum, but sometimes when he cries out, I think he's having nightmares." She rose and went to the door where they could talk quietly in the hall without fear of disturbing the child. "Brandley, I cannot tell you what a ninnyhammer I feel for causing so stupid a scene. I . . ."

He took both his sister's hands. "Don't blame yourself. I'll own it was a caper-witted thing to do. But why has Denton taken it into his head that it's *his* fault?"

"Oh, it was all nonsense. He led me a merry chase, and I vowed I'd get even. But Roberts was only supposed to hold up Denton on his way back — just frighten him a little — and then we'd laugh about it when he got home. I had no idea Peter would stowaway or that it would rain or that they'd arrive late, and he'd stop the whole coach.

"Oh, Brandley, it's such a terrible muddle — the Silberts frightened, Peter sick,

198

and you —" She put out her hand to her brother.

"I am a bit bruised, although not nearly so much as Peter. But I'm not such a cawker that a fall from a horse into a very soft puddle of mud cannot be borne. I'll sit with Peter now."

She opened her mouth to protest, but he took her firmly by the shoulder and turned her toward the stairs. "Now you go to your bed. I am not the least bit sleepy and may as well sit here as in my own room."

"But —"

"And what good will you be to Peter tomorrow when he really needs you if you go without a night of sleep?"

The argument silenced her, and she took two steps down the hall. Then she turned back. "Thank you, Brandley."

"Good night. My chance to return the favor for all those nights you sat over me."

Closing the door softly behind him, Brandley surveyed the small form in the middle of the big bed. Except for a bruise on his forehead, Peter was as white as the sheets and so still Brandley looked twice to be sure he was breathing. Brandley took the seat his sister had left and prepared for a long watch. Why hadn't he brought a book? But he didn't dare leave to get one in case

Peter should waken and need him.

Perhaps an hour later, the sleeping draught began to wear off. Peter became fretful, whimpering in his sleep. "Stop, stop. Ouch!" The patient tossed his head on the pillow, then suddenly opened his eyes, wide and staring. "I'm thirsty."

Brandley was beside him in a moment, lifting him to a sitting position and holding the glass of barley water to his lips. Peter drank half the glass. "Uncle Brandley? Where's Mama?"

"She's sleeping. I'll stay here awhile, and then she'll come back."

"You won't leave? Don't let the horses run."

"No, I won't leave, and you're quite safe. You were just having a bad dream. Go back to sleep." He laid the child on the pillow and smoothed the sheet before returning to his chair, glad that Peter had accepted his presence. Gwyneth had been so near collapse that he resolved not to call her unless absolutely necessary.

Peter stirred twice, then drifted back to sleep. For the watching Brandley, it was as if the years had rolled backward and he was the small white form in the bed, aching and restless. He was glad that Peter's illness didn't seem desperate, yet he felt the child's suffering as his own and would do all possible to stop it.

The fire flickered on the hearth, and Peter's breathing deepened. Brandley closed his eyes. In the state of semiconsciousness that followed, he saw again the dark clouds gathering over the moor and felt within himself the urgency to reach the carriage before harm could come to Peter. But as the clouds churned and boiled across the sky, it seemed that pieces broke off and floated higher, becoming white and fluffy, like Aristophanes' god clouds. And then the clouds formed around a high wooden structure like a pulpit, and a white-robed figure was exhorting from notes on a pink-tasseled cushion. The clouds rolled on, and Brandley came back to consciousness with a start as Peter turned and flung his covers off.

The child's hot forehead told Brandley the fever was mounting. He bathed the small face with lavender water and straightened the sheet. For a moment Peter seemed to grow quiet, but then he cried out more sharply than before. Brandley moved to sit on the edge of the bed and picked up a thin, hot hand. "Peter, you're all right. Try to rest." The gentle words spoken in a firm voice seemed to reach Peter. He stopped tossing his head. But when Brandley released his hand, the child whimpered again.

So Brandley settled himself on the bed and held his nephew's hand. In the quiet of the room he thought again about his dream. The figure in the pulpit must have been Simeon. Odd that the commencement sermon should have made such an impression on him. To help himself stay awake, he tried to recall the preacher's message. He'd paid scant attention to the words at the time, having focused more on the famous man himself.

It had been about prayer he remembered after some groping. But much mind-searching produced only one line: "Those who make light of prayers show that they know not what spirit they are of. . . ." Spirit . . . clouds . . . In the flickering light of the fire, images melded in Brandley's mind.

He might have sat there till morning holding Peter's hand had the patient not jerked restlessly and pulled away. With considerable relief to his own bruised and aching muscles, Brandley returned to the armchair. But only for a second. Peter muttered, "Thirsty." Brandley again moved to his side to give him a drink.

It was when he picked up the pitcher to pour the water that Brandley noticed the prayer book lying under a tattered storybook. Nana had been doing her duty in her reading to the children. When Peter pushed away the cup, Brandley picked up the book with more than idle curiosity. Peter's fever was increasing, and Brandley's concern grew. A simple cold, even pneumonia, he could be nursed through; but something more serious, like rheumatic fever, could leave the child weakened for life. Brandley knew so well what that meant. If there was a chance it would help, he might even be willing to pray.

The table of contents directed him to a prayer for a sick child.

Oh, Almighty God and merciful Father, to whom alone belong the issues of life and death; look down from heaven, we humbly beseech Thee, with the eyes of mercy upon this child now lying upon the bed of sickness: Visit him, Lord, with Thy salvation; deliver him in Thy good appointed time from his bodily pain and save his soul for Thy mercies' sake. . . .

Brandley closed the book. Seeking health and fitness was one thing, but praying for salvation seemed doing it rather too brown. He turned toward the front of the book and tried another prayer.

Oh, God, whose nature and property is ever to have mercy and to forgive, receive our humble petitions; and though we be tied and bound with the chains of our sins, yet let Thy great mercy loose us; for the honor of Jesus Christ, our Mediator and Advocate. Amen.

He closed the book. What forgiveness for sins had to say to the situation he couldn't see, but Peter was sleeping more easily.

Dr. Eliot nodded his head over his young patient the next morning and instructed them to continue plying Peter with barley water, lemonade, and tea. "Push the fluids," he told Gwyneth, who was calm and refreshed after the sleep her brother's nursing had allowed her. "I had thought to order a paregoric draught, but I am satisfied that won't be necessary." He pointed at Peter. "I'll be back tomorrow. I expect to see you looking much more the thing, young man."

The doctor's prognosis was correct. In spite of an uncomfortable day of fluctuating fever and chills and a restless night, the following day Peter was well enough to be taken to task by his father for his behavior.

"Peter, whatever possessed you?"

"I don't know, Father. Really, I don't.

Well, maybe I do a little. I thought it would be fun to hide away — I just fit in the box. I knew you were going along for a ways, and I thought we'd have a fine time coming home together. It was fun until the storm started, and then —" He struggled manfully against the tears at the back of his eyes.

"And why didn't you sit up or call for help?"

"I did once, but there was no one at the back to see me. No one heard me call, and the mud from the wheels kept hitting my face. It was better to stay under the lid. The rain kept off until the wind started blowing it in, and then the box filled with water."

"Yes, I believe I have the picture. Well, young man, I hope this will be the end of your escapades. You do as your mother and the doctor tell you now."

"Yes, sir."

After lunch Peter was propped up with cushions and allowed to play a game of snakes-and-ladders with Uncle Brandley. Only once, while sitting with Peter during an afternoon nap, did Brandley consider that the turning point that first night seemed to come after reading the prayers. Had God really heard and answered?

13

With Peter on the mend, the remaining weeks of summer seemed to slide downhill. Brandley kept busy with his endless reading interspersed with rides across the open moorland and several visits a day to the convalescent to read to him or play snakes-and-ladders. The neighborhood became much quieter when the Alluring Lurinda removed to Brighton after an unsuccessful attempt to convince Baronet Hilliard to accompany her.

The puppies were weaned and placed in new homes. Peter claimed Balin and Balan, and Gwyneth was so pleased with her son's returning health that he was even permitted to keep them in his room. The child knew better than to let his mother actually see them in bed with him, and she never commented on the little patches of dog hair on the bedclothes.

Amy liked Ulfis and Gwen the most, but she was sad at not being allowed to keep them all. Merlin was bestowed on a very pleased Dr. Midgeholme. This gave Brandley the idea of taking Galahad back to Cambridge with him to present to his friend Mr. Deighton, the bookseller.

When not attending her son, Gwyneth made inquiries at the registry office in York to locate a housekeeper for her brother. The first applicant she interviewed had dirty hair and fingernails. The second soon showed herself to be a compulsive talker. When applicant number three expressed doubts about serving as housekeeper to a pedantic bachelor who would litter a nice clean house with books and papers, Gwyneth began to despair.

Fortunately, three days later Nurse drove over from Fancourt bringing Carleton's eldest, Felix, just six months older than Peter, for a visit with his cousin. Gwyneth shared her problem.

"Bless ye, Miz Gwyneth, the Good Book tells us that we munnot worry over such things because the Lord Hisself will supply all our needs. My brother's girl, Molly, has been keeping house for our parson seven years now, but he's a fixing to go to the Colonies as a missionary. She'll know how to keep house for Mester Brandley well enou', I'll warrant."

Gwyneth was more inclined to think that the need had been supplied by Nurse rather than any Higher Authority. But instead of voicing such heresy, she simply reminded Nurse, "It's the United States now — not the Colonies. Almost fifty years since, you know."

"Eh! It's just as far away," replied Nurse with great practicality. "I'll bring Molly round Sunday after chapel. Tha'll see she's just what tha's a needing."

Indeed, Molly Hibbley *was* just what Gwyneth was looking for. The austere no-nonsense appearance of her sturdy build, scrubbed ruddy face, and tidy brown hair under a starched white cap was relieved by the twinkle in her eye that told Gwyneth that Molly would manage very well with her new master.

Molly had raised her sister and three brothers after their mother's death. Nine years later, when her sister married Tom, the carter's son, Molly secured a good position as housekeeper to Parson Adams. Now at thirty-one she was very pleased with this new position which the Good Lord, to whom she had dedicated her life under the parson's teaching, had provided for her.

As soon as all was arranged, Brandley bid farewell to the Okeford Hall family. With his groom and manservant, he drove to Cambridge the third week in August. Molly would follow by mail coach a fortnight later, by which time Brandley expected to have located a residence.

But after ten days in Cambridge, that plan seemed overly optimistic. Brandley had even less patience with house-hunting than most young men of his age, and the job was becoming increasingly irritating.

"No," he informed the agent, "I do not require 'a delightful family house enjoying a magnificent outlook across Coe Fen' nor a 'lovely period house in a superb parkland setting providing complete peace and seclusion.'"

However, a three-room flat above the chemist's was hardly acceptable either. Wasn't there an agent in all of Cambridgeshire offering a pleasant residence with an adequate stable?

Returning to the inn from an exceptionally frustrating afternoon with the agent, Brandley was surprised to find Dr. Silbert. "Thought it was time you were back in Cambridge so I dropped around. The innkeeper suggested I wait." He shook Brandley's hand heartily. "Won't you come home for supper with me? My wife and I find the evenings rather lonesome since Elinor has gone to Bath with her aunt."

Hearing that Elinor was gone, he accepted the invitation. Over dinner Dr. Silbert took great delight in telling about his research expedition after leaving Okeford. "Tiny Clitheroe, the smallest castle in England, was well worth the climb to the summit of the limestone hill on which it perched. Since the day following the fateful rainstorm was fine, we enjoyed scrambling all over the surviving keep with its flat, square corner towers, one of which surprised us with a spiral staircase inside.

"Tutbury, whose decaying walls had been restored by John of Gaunt himself, was eclipsed by the red stone magnificence of Kenilworth, the Duke of Lancaster's favorite castle. Although much had been destroyed in Cromwell's time when Parliamentary forces blew up part of the massive keep, John of Gaunt's hall can still be seen."

As soon as they left the table, Mrs. Silbert brought out her sketches of each site and added her comments. Brandley was impressed by his friends' careful investigation, and it was pleasant to spend the evening in a home instead of at The Sun, which he was beginning to despair of ever being able to abandon. Perhaps he should accept the appointment that had been offered him to become a Trinity fellow and move into a college living. Of course, that would mean he would have to remain single, but there didn't seem to be much of an obstacle to that.

After returning her sketchbook to its shelf, Mrs. Silbert produced Elinor's latest letter. She would remain in Bath with her aunt and cousin until the end of the season as Mrs. Silbert's sister-in-law was finding the waters even more beneficial than her physician had hoped. Elinor and her eighteen-year-old cousin Clarissa were in a whirl of assemblies, musicales, and theater parties. Mrs. Silbert was telling about the Pump Room meetings, promenade walks, and tea parties at the Royal Crescent when Katy brought their tea.

"Have you inquired about housing at the university office?" Professor Silbert asked. "They often have listings not available to other agents — from people who prefer to sell or rent to someone connected with the university."

Brandley was not even aware of such a service. With this new lead he renewed his efforts after breakfast the next morning. Having steeled himself to disappointment, the surprise of finding three respectable houses in the university district almost overwhelmed him. So it was that before nuncheon he had just the right place to suit his needs and had arranged for the carrier to move him on the following day. The gracious old house with half-timbered beams and a slate roof fronted by three dormers had been built in the days of James I, but had undergone its latest modernization only three years before. Brandley was grateful to be away from the noise and bustle of a busy inn. Barrow expressed his pleasure with the stable and immediately began making a home for the horses and dogs even before unpacking his own trunk, while Croydon gave all his master's boots a champagne polish to mark the occasion.

The find came none too soon, for the next day Molly Hibbley arrived. But even the unflappable Molly was not prepared for the glories of modernization. "Mester Brandley, a Robinson stove! What a luxury! Makes a body wonder what they'll think of next. And a WC. Bless me!" Molly came the closest she ever had to giggling in all her sensible life.

"The residence was formerly owned by a well-to-do gentleman who believed in providing himself with comforts. But because he traveled a great deal, he couldn't see keeping up a large estate in his absence," Brandley explained.

"Aye, and he believed in providing his help with comforts too." Molly bent over to touch the Robinson stove reverently. The cast-iron contraption had side panels that could be wound up to reduce the size of the open fire in the center, a roasting oven beside the flame, and grills on top for frying or boiling. Molly couldn't wait to cook her first meal.

Three days later Brandley was still unpacking and sorting books in his library when he came across a volume loaned to him by Professor Silbert, packed away by mistake last spring. He laid it aside, thinking he would return it later, when a glance out the window convinced him that this would be a perfect day for a ride. Emrys was getting restless in his small paddock anyway.

Riding along Trumpington Street, Brandley took in the seasonal changes. Lavender fall crocuses bloomed in the yards under an autumn sky of pale blue with wispy clouds. The trees still wore their summer green, but the ivy on Pembroke College across from Peterhouse was a brilliant contrast — half still a fresh green, half turned to rust, red, and deep purple. It was a sure sign that Cambridge had been enjoying cold nights and sunny days.

Turning his thoughts inward, Brandley recalled his last evening with the Silberts. He realized that this was the first time he'd had the leisure to reflect on the uneasiness he had felt when Mrs. Silbert outlined Elinor's holiday to him — Elinor dancing at assemblies, Elinor on the promenade, Elinor at a theater party — with her aunt and cousin, and who else? Then he knew why the apprehension had stubbornly remained even when the subject wasn't consciously on his mind. Jack was in Bath. Charlie had told him that in the same breath with which he had said Jack would offer for Elinor.

He would have to get used to it, he told himself, go right on building the life he had always expected to live — studies and lectures, writing, horses and dogs, summers and Christmases with Gwyneth and Calvert. Funny, that had always seemed the epitome of happiness until he met Elinor. Well, he had always said he wouldn't marry.

Marry! He'd never really looked at it quite that way. Did he really think Elinor would marry him even if Jack weren't on the scene? She was so lively and graceful, spending her holiday dancing at this very moment. His mind filled with scenes of women in graceful swirling skirts and bowing tail-coated gentlemen beneath crystal chandeliers. He could hardly think she would want a cripple for a husband. She seemed further beyond his reach each time he looked.

True, she did seem to enjoy his company, but . . . He could hope for a small income from royalties on his publications, and even though he allowed Carleton most of the income from the estate, he had an adequate income from his father's will — enough to provide every comfort even if he took a wife. But it was paltry next to the Widkham fortunes.

So where did all this leave him? Well, it wasn't as if he had any choice. No reason to give up his friendship with the Silberts though. Elinor would be living at Ranswood Park and London and Bath. Not much chance she'd be around here often to disturb his peace. He always came back to that — as if he had any to disturb.

Brandley's cynical reflections ended as he drew rein at the Silbert home. Mrs. Silbert welcomed him warmly herself today since Katy was busy in the kitchen. She was delighted to hear about his house and wanted all the details.

"Well, why don't you and Dr. Silbert drive over tomorrow and see for yourself — especially the wonderful Robinson stove?"

"We would love to. And now won't you stay for tea?"

Since Brandley had eaten only an apple and a piece of cheese for lunch, he was glad for the invitation — even though it meant hearing Elinor's latest letter about Mr.

Sheridan's play, about the ball at the New Assembly Rooms, and the Harmonic Society Glee at the White Hart.

"She asks if you are back in Cambridge yet and if you've found a house. After I see it tomorrow, I shall be able to send her all the details. Her uncle plans to return her to us in a fortnight." Mrs. Silbert refolded the letter and laid it aside.

The next day the Silberts arrived for tea and their tour. "Brandley, it's enchanting." Mrs. Silbert beamed her approval. "And the modernization hasn't spoiled its character at all."

In the library the professor and his host were immediately drawn to the shelves of books while Mrs. Silbert admired the stonework in the fireplace and the rust and beige Chippendale sofa which repeated the colors of the stone and brightened the dark wood of the walls and shelves. "I am glad the improver stopped short of adding gas lighting," she said, noting the balanced proportions of the brass sconces on either side of the fireplace.

They then moved into the garden. "It's delightful. So late in the summer and still so much color. I can almost feel the brushes in my hand." Mrs. Silbert surveyed the flower beds surrounding the small lawn, ablaze with geraniums, hollyhocks, and Canterbury bells.

"I fear they need a caring hand to remove the weeds. I'm not much of a gardener — much as I do enjoy having flowers." Brandley grinned ruefully.

"Would you like me to send Wattle around when he looks after our garden on Thursday?" asked Dr. Silbert.

"Indeed, I would like it very much. Thank you for your kindness."

Brandley's domestic staff was now complete, and he was free to give his full attention to settling into his new life. He saw the Silberts frequently and twice enjoyed evening dinners followed by chess, a progress report on the professor's book, and the inevitable snatches from Elinor's letters.

The days were pleasant enough with plenty of time to proofread the galleys of his book from the University Press and to begin research on his next project. He was glad to have his dogs with him again, and Molly proved to be the capable housekeeper Nurse had promised.

It was in the evenings, whether after dinner at the Silberts or spent quietly by himself, that Brandley came face to face with the reality that his new home could be lonesome and that even his favorite books weren't always the solution. It was on one such evening, made more dismal by the wind and drizzling rain blowing against his library window, that Brandley invited Molly to take a cup with him when she brought in tea.

"Aye, the wind is wuthering tonight, sir."

He smiled at the comforting moorland phrase. "Indeed it is. And how do you fancy Cambridge, Mrs. Hibbley?" He used the name Calvert had bestowed on her likewise unmarried aunt as a gesture of respect.

"Eh! Graidely, Mester Brandley." She recounted the special joys she had found here, especially Market Hill. It sprang to bustling life every Wednesday with the natural exuberance of an overcrowded country-town market, the streets "so busy they fair scuffle." She took a drink of tea and then went on to tell him of Sunday services at Holy Trinity Church.

Brandley was greatly surprised that his nonconformist housekeeper should be attending services at an Anglican church. Then he remembered that the pastor there was Charles Simeon. Apparently it was true, as he had heard, that Simeon's preaching appealed to the poor and unlearned as well as to the educated minds of Cambridge scholars.

"Holy Trinity? Isn't that quite a change from your parson's chapel?" He tried to show polite interest without condescension.

"Well, Mester Brandley, Charles Simeon's none a Methodist, but he's a man of God sure as I'm sitting here. There's them as calls him an evangelical Anglican."

The unfamiliar phrase on her Yorkshire tongue caught Brandley's attention and made him smile. He sipped his tea. "And what does the singular Mr. Simeon preach about that is so appealing?" How was it possible to reach so wide a diversity of classes in one sermon? The only sermon he had heard from the preacher had been directed to the academic community.

The evangelist in Molly seized the opportunity. "Eh, sir, he ses sin is rebellion against God as our benefactor — that sin brings pain and sorrow and Hell for all as die without the love of God in their hearts." She spoke her words very carefully.

"Very gloomy, I must say — sin and damnation. What are we supposed to do about our crimes against the Divine?" His off-handed attitude stopped just short of impertinence. He leaned back in his chair recalling the line from *The Clouds*: "Heaven is one vast fire-extinguisher."

"Now, Mester Brandley, that's just the point. *We* canna' do anything. Man is a poor helpless creature that canna' change hisself or make his peace." She paused gravely, then continued eagerly, her eyes shining. "Pardon and holiness mun come of the Savior. The treasures of grace are in Jesus Christ for the use of poor and needy sinners, and He is full of love as well as power."

Brandley was amused and impressed by her fluency. "Well spoken, Mrs. Hibbley. How did you come by such a fancy phrase as 'treasures of grace'? Were you drilled?" He raised his eyebrows with just the hint of a grin.

"Eh! I was much struck by it in last Sunday's sermon, sir. Mester Simeon ses a body should seek His grace directly and diligently, and all as seeks shall find the salvation of God." She accompanied her words with an earnest nodding of her head, her dialect almost vanishing as she quoted.

There didn't seem to be much to reply to this, so Brandley turned his attention to finishing his tea. Molly followed his example and left to wash up.

The conversation was unsettling to Brandley. His religious experience — beyond the twice-daily compulsory chapel services at

Trinity — had amounted to accompanying Gwyneth to Harvest Home Service and to church on Sundays when the weather did not permit hunting or fishing. They were accustomed to hearing Dr. Midgeholme deliver a reasonable theological essay of a sermon, spoken in a perfectly boring tone. Teaching on loving one's brother and visiting the orphaned and widowed were well enough, but the miracles were awkward material. After all, in this enlightened age it was understood that reason was the point at which God touched man. One had to be rather careful about a "revealed" religion. The Vicar of Thirsk could certainly never be accused of enthusiasm.

In a lifetime of casual churchgoing, Brandley had encountered much stateliness, precision, and carefully worked out elegance, all with a distinct want of flexibility, familiarity, or humanness. Christian discourse was discreetly aloof from life. Nothing in his background prepared Brandley to accept the need of a personal Savior. Yet, as an intellectual inquiry, the subject was intriguing.

Long after blowing out his candle, he was thinking of his conversation with Molly. Was there really a God beyond the clouds who cared about him personally, who offered love and help in his daily problems? He doubted it. But it was obviously a helpful belief for Molly. He was glad she was happy. Her cheerfulness made his home less somber.

He had almost drifted off to sleep when he came back to consciousness with a start. Tomorrow was Saturday, the day Elinor was to return home. And he had unthinkingly accepted Mrs. Silbert's invitation for tea. He thought of Elinor returning bright and sparkling from her whirl of parties — undoubtedly betrothed to Jack. He minded the thought of that worse than anything he had ever faced in his life. And he hated minding. He realized how desperately he wanted what he could never have. And he despised himself for wanting it.

14

After a few hours of restless sleep, Brandley awoke. He lay in bed awhile, trying to sort out the source of the confusion he felt, sleep clouding his mind. It had been a pleasant enough evening, the loneliness held at bay by Mrs. Hibbley. Then he remembered. Elinor was coming home today, and he was going to see her. Hearing of her engagement would be bad enough under any circumstances, but after their last parting . . .

He sat with his head in his hands. He couldn't face her. He'd send a boy around with a note to Mrs. Silbert. He would think of some excuse. Yet he had to face her sometime. Delay only made it worse. Well, he'd never run shy yet, although he had considered it. He'd stand buff.

Brandley took his usual morning coffee with toast and then returned to his work, closeting himself in his library. He pared a quill, determined to do something useful with the time until his engagement with the Silberts. He was soon sufficiently absorbed in his notes on Roman history and law that when Molly knocked to ask if he would take nuncheon on a tray in the library, it seemed impossible that the morning was gone. He continued working as he ate and was able to leave the library two hours later with the feeling of having accomplished a tidy piece of work.

So it was that he approached the Silberts in better spirits than he had expected. When Elinor opened the door, it was obvious that her spirits were in no need of raising. She stood in the doorway — sweet, radiant, incredibly dear. The smiling welcome, the outstretched hands banished any worries Brandley had about their parting scene last July. At least Elinor was not holding his outburst in the arbor against him, nor apparently thinking poorly of him for the ridiculous figure he had cut later.

As Brandley was introduced to Uncle Phillips, Mustard trotted up, wanting her ears scratched. Brandley had little appetite for tea, but in spite of himself he enjoyed Elinor's bright recounting of the delights of Bath.

Elinor was too wrapped up in sharing her adventures to drink her tea either. It cooled in her cup as she told with animation of the harpsichordist who played Handel and the chamber group that performed Mozart with such feeling.

As she chatted brightly, answering questions from her parents, who were obviously delighted to have their daughter with them again, Brandley had to admit that she was even more beautiful than he remembered — her hair more golden and her smile brighter. So apparently the social whirl did agree with her just as Charlie had predicted. Jack's name had still not come up. Brandley supposed she was waiting for Lord Widkham to speak to her father. Well, he wished they'd get it over with.

Tea was finished — at least Uncle Phillips and Dr. Silbert had done it justice — and Elinor's father took his brother-in-law off to the library.

"Dear, you must see the chrysanthemums," insisted Mrs. Silbert. "They are in full bloom now and more beautiful than I've ever seen them."

"Yes, Brandley, let's do go for a stroll." Elinor jumped up and led the way into the golden late summer afternoon.

The chrysanthemums were a blaze of amber, bronze, and rust, the garden bench where they sat last spring as inviting as ever, the sun adding gilt patterns on the lawn between the lengthening shadows. Squirrels, making frantic attempts to fill their nests for the approaching winter, rustled and chattered in the flower beds, and the delicate scent of clematis was just perceptible on the still air.

"So you've become quite the toast of the ton, it seems." He winced. He hadn't meant to sound so caustic.

She tactfully ignored his tone. "Well, not quite of the *first* stare. But it was fun." She smiled a bit dreamily. "I think every girl should have one season even if it is only in Bath. It wouldn't do to go through the rest of one's life wondering what one had missed."

Brandley's heart skipped a beat. "*One* season?"

"Oh, yes. One was quite enough. Do you realize that some people *live* that way — their whole lives? Just going from the London season, to parties at country houses, to Brighton or Bath," she finished with something like a shudder. "I took six books with me and didn't finish one." And with that she sat quietly looking at Brandley. It was clearly his turn.

The erudite Brandley was not often at a loss for words, but this, so beyond anything he dared to hope for, left him quite dumbfounded. He stammered, "But Jack . . . I mean . . . I'm making a shocking mull of this, but —" Groping to express himself, he rose from the bench.

"Oh, yes, Jack was there. Very much there." She teased him with her smile. "He offered for me, you know."

He took it on his feet. He knew it was coming. He thought he was prepared. The wound was unbearable. He rigidly controlled his features. His hands clenched until the nails bit into his flesh.

"Brandley! Don't look like that!" The teasing was gone now. "Brandley, I —"

The French windows from the dining parlor opened with a clatter, and Katy ushered a glowing Lady Lurinda into the scene. With a whirl of taffeta skirts in shades of bronze, cinnamon, and russet that made the backdrop of chrysanthemums look like a stage set designed especially for her, she crossed to Brandley holding out her hand.

"Sir Brandley, your housekeeper told me I might find you here. It has been ages since we parted. I simply couldn't wait. I have been quite in the sullens ever since you so heartlessly refused to accompany me to Brighton."

Brandley bowed over the hand extended to him. "I believe you have made the acquaintance of Miss Elinor Silbert, Lady Lurinda Ormsby."

The women nodded to one another, Lurinda with an offhanded toss of her head that made the fetching little feather on her hat shine in the sun, Elinor with an abrupt coldness that would have told Brandley what she thought of the *Ne Plus Ultra* if he had noticed.

"And what happy circumstance brings you to Cambridgeshire, My Lady?" Brandley offered his arm to Lurinda. He must get away from Elinor — from Jack's fiancée.

They began walking slowly toward the door. "Family duties. My brother Gerald has become betrothed to a dear child whose family seat is just a few miles from here. I have accepted her mother's invitation for a visit, and, of course, I couldn't think of coming so near without calling on you."

At the door Brandley paused, turned, and bowed his farewell to Elinor. "Please accept my felicitations, Miss Silbert, and convey my farewell to your parents."

Even from that distance Elinor could see the stony set of his features. She wanted to cry out, to make them stop, to force Brandley to listen to her. Then doubt followed on the heels of desperation. Perhaps Lurinda had a right to be possessive. She and Brandley had been near neighbors and good friends all summer. Lurinda *was* alluring, and she was making no secret of the fact that she had set her cap at Brandley. Well, if that was the way it was supposed to be, it was fortunate for Elinor that her speech had been stopped.

The next morning, however, a sleepless night had determined Elinor to set the record straight. If Brandley had chosen Lady Lurinda — and Elinor was convinced he had — that was his affair. But she would not be denied the right to speak her piece. The more she thought about it, the more determined she became.

Taking extra care with her appearance, Elinor chose a light green dress with a wide border of green leaves worked around the hem and up one side of the skirt. Aunt Phillips had ordered it for Elinor from her dressmaker in Bath, and it had been much admired there. Because it was a cool morning, she chose a dark green velvet Spencer jacket that ended at her tiny waist and a poke bonnet wreathed with green leaves and clusters of tangerine berries. All the time she was dressing, her irritation grew. He had actually walked out on her in the middle of a sentence. Well, Sir Brandley Hilliard, Bart., was going to hear the rest of that sentence if they were the last words he ever heard from her lips.

"Katy, please ask Cobbett to harness the

carriage. I am going out." It was unusual for Elinor to summon the carriage since she normally preferred riding or walking. But this morning she would arrive at her destination as a lady. She even considered asking Katy to accompany her, but then she decided that would be doing it rather too brown.

Before Elinor could leave, however, Katy entered to announce Faith and Hope Underhill accompanied by Miss Rashton. In a flurry of ruffled petticoats the girls couldn't even wait for Katy to bring the tea tray before bursting forth with their news.

"Have you heard the latest on dit?"

"Isn't it just the most famous thing imaginable?"

"Mama says with Lady Ormsby's looks and Sir Brandley's brains, they should be happy as grigs."

With concentrated effort Elinor poured the tea and managed to drink her cup to the bottom without the contents sloshing so much as once. Setting her cup aside, she rose and smoothed her skirt. "I know you will forgive my abrupt departure, but I was just about to pay a call when you arrived. Mother will serve you another cup of tea." Elinor left the room.

As the Silbert carriage pulled up in front of the baronet's house, the mullioned windows of the second story of the half-timbered house sparkled in the morning sun, testimony to Molly's devoted efforts. Her back straight, her head high, Elinor walked to the door and pulled the bell with determination.

Still tucking stray hairs under her dust cap, Molly opened the door. "Will you please inform Sir Brandley that Miss Silbert has come to call." Elinor's voice was steady.

"Eh, and I'm sure he'd be graidely pleased to see tha', but he's gone riding with Lady Ormsby. Would tha' care to wait?"

"No, thank you. When your master returns, you may inform him I called." Elinor turned sharply and was halfway down the path when a familiar voice stopped her.

"Dash it all, Elinor, never saw you in such high ropes before."

"Charlie!" She turned, delighted to see his smiling face. She was sorely in need of someone to talk to.

"Wise not to wait. Been kicking my heels here an hour already myself."

"Do you have your horse, or may I offer you a ride?" Elinor asked.

"Walked over. Dashed silly thing to do. Got my boots beastly dirty. Not that you could see your face in 'em to start with, of course." He grinned as he handed her into the carriage and got in beside her.

Charlie looked Elinor and the carriage over. "Making a formal call on old Hilliard?"

Elinor raised her chin and forced a smile. "Certainly. I intended to wish him well on his attachment to Lady Ormsby."

Charlie looked struck and then exploded, "The *Ne Plus Ultra!* Hilliard! Anyone would think you'd been in the sun." He was silent for a moment. "Oh, I daresay you're hoaxing me."

"I am not hoaxing you. My felicitations may be a bit premature, but I am quite in earnest."

"Brandley Hilliard and Lady Lurinda Ormsby?" Charlie sat dumbfounded shaking his head. "What a dashed loose-screw thing to do." His silent contemplation continued, the clip-clop of the horse's hooves the only sound. "I smell a bubble. Tell you what — I promised Hilliard I'd do him a good turn. Looks like the right time. I'll give a soiree."

"Charlie!" Now it was Elinor's turn to be dumbfounded. The thought of Charlie as a social leader was beyond her powers of imagination.

But once determined on a course of action, Charlie was unshakable. He could not untangle this hubble-bubble, but he had no doubt that it was simply a misunderstanding that could be solved by bringing the principal parties together. And he would host the social function where it should be accomplished. Two days later his card arrived, requesting the presence of Dr. and Mrs. Silbert and Miss Elinor Silbert at a levee in private rooms at The Sun on Thursday next.

Determined to hold her own against Lurinda, Elinor chose a maize silk dress with a deep flounce of Mechlin lace at the hem, which had also been a gift from Aunt Phillips. When Katy completed dressing her hair with a circlet of French silk roses and fastening a necklace of gold filigree around her neck, Elinor was satisfied with her appearance.

As soon as they arrived at The Sun, Dr. Silbert made his way to the card room Charlie had provided for the entertainment of the elder gentlemen. Mrs. Silbert was claimed for a tete-a-tete by Mrs. Underhill. Even before she could get her bearings, Elinor was surrounded by the Misses Underhill — Faith, Hope, and Charity too, who was now deemed old enough to take part in social activities.

"Have you *seen* her?" Faith bobbed her curls.

"Just think, a diamond of the first water in Cambridge." Charity giggled.

Not wanting to hear any more of their chatter, Elinor turned just in time to see the Alluring Lurinda make her entrance on the arm of the baronet. Lady Ormsby was radiant in heavy peach taffeta. Her burnished auburn locks were dressed in the latest French manner with embroidered white organdy frills, white roses with green foliage, and peach gauze ribbon. The ribbons fluttered from the cluster of curls over each ear to rest charmingly on her bare shoulders.

But to Elinor's eye, Lurinda's escort was an even more arresting sight. Under his perfectly cut long-tailed brown evening coat, he wore a cream waistcoat with a gold chain. His snowy shirt, topped with a meticulously tied cravat, revealed a small row of ruffles beneath each cuff. Fawn-colored pantaloons were fastened at the ankle with rows of small brass buttons above black pumps. Elinor caught her breath. She had become so accustomed to thinking of him as a lonely little boy, an unhappy man, and a dear companion that she had forgotten the distinction he had attained.

"Oh, come, let's have a glass of punch before the room is an absolute squeeze." Faith Underhill tugged at Elinor's sleeve. Elinor gratefully turned from the disturbing scene.

"Isn't Lord Widkham here?" Charity craned her neck to observe all the guests. "I've heard he's absolutely top-of-the-trees."

"Charity, you must stop using that vulgar cant. I have no notion where you could have picked it up."

The sisterly squabble continued as Elinor sipped her punch. Charlie had managed on very short notice to fill his rented rooms with gownsmen and friends from the community, so Elinor found no difficulty in keeping her distance from the couple that seemed to be the center of everyone's attention. But she was hoping her papa wasn't too deeply engrossed in a cribbage game as she would like to make her escape soon. No. She scolded herself sharply. She had come to speak to Sir Brandley, and she would not leave without doing so.

Just as the cold supper was being served, Jack made his entrance in a brilliant king's blue coat with gleaming gold buttons and an exquisite waterfall-tied cravat above a white French silk waistcoat. He came straight to Elinor and bowed with a flourish.

Elinor had just accepted his arm when a slightly red-faced Charlie approached them. "There you are, Widkham. What kept you? Afraid I'd gone to all this trouble for nothing. Come along now. I want you to meet a friend of mine."

Raising one eyebrow, Jack obediently followed, explaining to Elinor as they made their way across the crowded room, "Big meet at Newmarket today. Couldn't leave while Dame Fortune was smiling. This was my lucky day."

"No idea how lucky." Charlie turned back to him and then stopped. Brandley and Lurinda were just ready to serve themselves from the buffet when he accosted them. "Lady Lurinda, may I present the Marquess of Widkham. Lord Widkham, the *Ne Plus Ultra.*"

For three full seconds the principals of the scene stared at one another. Charlie, unsure what to do next, started to stammer something. But Brandley, perfectly at ease, took command with a current of humor just beneath the surface. "I believe it's customary to bow to the lady, Jack." He gently took Lurinda's hand from his arm and extended it toward the marquess.

As if he had suddenly wakened from a deep daydream, Jack made the most magnificent bow ever executed in The Sun. The Alluring Lurinda almost curtsied in response. As they moved off through the crowded room, the guests parted for them like the Red Sea.

"It would seem," Brandley commented wryly, "that an English marquess is quite as good as a French marquis."

"Tell you what," Charlie said, beaming at the success of his scheme, "it's better."

"Charles, whatever was that all about?" Faith Underhill claimed their host. "Did you see the way they looked at each other? It's *so* romantic."

As the pair moved off, Brandley turned to Elinor standing quietly at his elbow. He placed his hand gently on her elbow. "Elinor, I didn't think . . . what you must be enduring. May I get you a glass of punch?"

"Sir, there is a small garden at the rear of the inn. You may escort me there."

The secluded garden was surrounded by a high ivy-covered wall. Candlelight shining from the numerous windows of the inn made wavering golden patches on the lawn and bushes as Brandley and Elinor stepped into the fresh air.

"I can't imagine how Jack could behave with such impropriety toward you. But I must say you have borne it extremely well. May I hope to comfort you?" His offer was somewhat stiff but nonetheless sincere.

"What you may do, sir, is listen to me!" She pushed back the fear that Brandley really cared about Lurinda. "As I was trying to say when I was so rudely interrupted six days ago, Jack offered for me. But I refused him."

"You refused Lord Widkham? Elinor, is that . . . is that possible?" He turned to her, taking both her hands in his and shaking his head to clear the lightheaded feeling.

"Not only possible, but absolutely necessary. You must know, Daphne refused any number of handsome and eligible suitors. Jack's a very good friend. A bit overbearing at times perhaps, but quite good company. That's not a reason to marry the man though. After all, I could hardly marry him when I'm in love with someone else." Her lips curved in an inviting smile, and the softness in her eyes left no doubt as to the meaning of her words.

Brandley looked deeply into her eyes, and his whole life opened up in a blaze of ecstasy. He gathered her in his arms and bestowed on her lips the kiss he thought he would never have a right to give. It was a very gentle kiss as he savored the softness and sweetness of her mouth. She gave an inarticulate little sound between a sob and a laugh and hid her face against his shoulder.

"If you only knew how I've dreamt of this," he murmured in her ear. "You know, dearest, Daphne was Apollo's first love too."

Then he crushed her against him and kissed her again, more firmly this time, and she returned it with matching ardor as equal halves of one whole that come together after a lifetime of searching.

15

Elinor went to bed accompanied by the trill of crickets. She lay very still with her eyes closed and a tiny smile on her lips, savoring her happiness. She had been in love with Brandley for months, ever since that glowing June evening in their library when she sat beside him at the chessboard. She hugged the memory. At long last they had spoken their love — and Brandley had kissed her. If she lay very quiet, she could still feel his arms around her and his lips on hers. With a rush it all bubbled up inside her. She wanted to shout and laugh and cry.

She jumped out of bed, threw a shawl around her shoulders, and ran to her mother's room. "Oh, Mama, I'm sorry to waken you, but I shall simply burst if I have to contain it any longer!" The whole happy story tumbled around Mrs. Silbert's drowsy ears. "And Sunday we are to take nuncheon at his house. You and I must contrive to visit the gardens together so he and Papa can be undisturbed. Papa *will* give his consent, won't he?" They talked until the first notes of the lark warned of the sun's imminent approach.

In his country house on the other side of the Cam, Brandley was finding the night far less blissful. The initial shock of joy had begun to wear off, and he was stunned to find the ghost of old fears returning. Even so quickly could doubts set in? Could such overwhelming bliss be so ephemeral? No matter how he argued with himself, anxieties forced themselves on him. Elinor hadn't cared much for the assemblies at Bath, but mightn't she long for at least a country dance later? And what if his disability worsened as those things often did later in life? Was it fair to saddle such a lively creature with a cripple? It was indeed a jolt to discover that even Elinor's love had not erased his misgivings. If she could accept their future, why couldn't he? He could imagine nothing more sublime than sharing every day with her. Why should he doubt that this was enough? What more could life possibly offer? The uneasiness remained until sleep finally overcame his troubled thoughts.

By Sunday morning, however, only a slight suggestion of the somber reflections remained. This was the day appointed by Brandley to host a luncheon for the Silbert family — his first time to invite Elinor to his home. More immediate concerns eclipsed all other thoughts.

"Mrs. Hibbley, Mrs. Hibbley!" She bustled in with his coffee, not at all accustomed to receiving so peremptory a summons before breakfast.

"You aren't planning to go to services, are you? We have guests coming for nuncheon."

"Bless you, Mester Brandley, sir. So tha' told me last night. And the day before that. Everything's ready. Don't tha' fret. I'll be back in plenty of time to see to it all."

Her unruffled calm reassured Brandley, and he enjoyed his coffee and toast while listening to the chiming church bells.

When Brandley's guests arrived, he was able to match Elinor's radiating joy. Dr. and Mrs. Silbert might as well have been in another room. "It's the way they look at each other," Mrs. Silbert murmured to her husband, blinking her own misty eyes. "How well I remember just such a feeling, my love."

They enjoyed Molly's roast chicken (done to a turn on the prized Robinson stove), gallantine, jellies, and treacle tart — a much richer meal than she would have prepared for her master.

When no one could consume another purple grape or morsel of tangy cheese, Mrs. Silbert smiled at her daughter. "Why don't we take a turn in the garden now that Wattle has pulled all the weeds?"

They had waited only a short time when the men emerged from the house, shook hands for a final time, and joined them. "I have given this fellow leave to make his addresses to you, my dear." Dr. Silbert smiled at his daughter. "You must do as you think best, but I warned him he was in gravest danger of being sent packing."

A smiling Brandley offered his arm to Elinor as her parents withdrew to the parlor. Brandley wasn't sure whether he loved Elinor most as a serious student, an enchanted little girl, or a refined woman. He just knew he was very glad she was all that she was. She picked a bouquet of small lavender Michaelmas daisies while he basked in her beauty and joy.

She smiled at him, returning to the bench where he sat. Then after another blissful silence — it seemed they needed the space just to breathe in their happiness — Brandley spoke. "Did your parents send you to Bath to prevent our attachment?"

"Darling Brandley." She shook her head with a small laugh. "It was entirely the opposite. They think you are quite the thing. Nearly as far gone as their daughter."

"But then —"

"Slowtop! They knew how unsuitable such a life would be for me. They wanted to be sure I knew it too. Far from trying to keep us apart, they were pushing us together! Not that I needed any pushing," she finished almost shyly.

He took her in his arms again, and they sat together, the radiance of their love outshining the early autumn sun. Until a noise beyond the garden wall reminded them they weren't alone in the world. Elinor broke the silence to ask Brandley about his work. "I haven't heard a word about it since I got back."

So Brandley told her about the polishing touches on his manuscript and his ideas for a new book on the development of Roman law. "It's curious, but that all seems rather remote to me now. It was my whole life for so long." He rested a loving look on her.

"Am I a dreadful distraction?"

"Mmmm, a diverting indispensability, I should say. But what of *your* pursuits? Finished that one book you started in Bath yet? What is it, more Richard III?" The scene in the Okeford arbor was still a raw memory to him, but it wasn't hard to allude even to such unpleasantness now with their love to smooth the way.

"No, Henry V. He had a valiant noble

you'd like, Ralph Neville, Earl of Westmorland. He was hip-halt too." She said it almost like a caress, and the realization overwhelmed him. How could she be so casual about something so abhorrent?

"You really *don't* mind, do you?" His tone was utter wonderment.

She smiled and shook her head. "No, Brandley. I really *don't* mind. It's part of you — and I love you." He took her in his arms. She smiled at him, and he gave her the kiss they were both longing for, but a very brief one, as they heard the professor coming for his daughter. Brandley then had to take leave of his love somewhat publicly, with just a tightly squeezed hand and fond look as he handed her into the carriage.

The following day he went to see the Silberts and felt heartily welcomed into the family of which he had already become a vital part. Now they could share the news. Mrs. Silbert would send a notice to the newspaper. Brandley wrote to Gwyneth and Calvert. He knew they would be pleased. And Carleton should be informed too, he supposed. Oh well, Gwyneth could tell him. Elinor had written to her sister. Joan was already planning to visit them the following week, but Elinor couldn't wait that long to share the news.

Molly was delighted at the prospect of having a bride in the house. She knew how lonely winter evenings in a bachelor establishment could be. In her practical way, she showed her pleasure by vigorously polishing the furniture with cabinetmaker's wax until it gleamed.

Charlie's frequent visits and his bounding corgis were a source of endless pleasure to Molly even though she scolded him for his mannerless dogs, his muddy boots, and his crooked neck cloth. His pleasure and self-satisfaction in Brandley's happiness moved him to begin visiting the Madingley rectory with increased regularity.

Elinor and her mother spent many happy hours preparing her trousseau, trimming bonnets with ribbons and embellishing white linen undergarments with tatting and white silk embroidery. The shirred yoke of her delicate ecru nightshift required hours of tiny stitches, but Elinor sighed and hugged herself with anticipation, feeling all fluttery inside every time she surveyed the carefully folded piles of finery she would wear for her husband.

In all the bustle, Brandley found little time for reflection. Occasionally, however, a shadow of doubt or fear would reassert itself. How was it possible there should remain even a small emptiness? What else could he possibly want? He went over the same ground for the hundredth time. He had the academic honors he had considered the epitome of his hopes, but they left him unfulfilled. His bout of social success had been a pleasant amusement, but merely that. Winning Elinor's love had brought joy beyond his dreams. Yet in his questionings, he always came back to the same place — if Elinor could love him so totally, without reservation, why couldn't he accept himself?

Elinor's sister arrived the following week. Brandley, present with the family to greet her, saw that Joan was a taller, darker, more mature version of Elinor. The tranquility Elinor had told him about seemed to radiate in her serene smile and eyes.

"She approves," Elinor whispered to Brandley after dinner that evening.

"That's a relief. I suppose I should have been obliged to cry off if she hadn't." He replied with that crooked grin Elinor found so endearing as it revealed the boyishness that lurked behind the man. It made her happy to see how the lines in his face had softened in the last two weeks. She rarely saw the bitter self-mocking look in his eyes any more, but it hurt her deeply when she did. It had been there before Joan came into the parlor to meet him, and Elinor knew he was fighting the old dread of meeting strangers. Joan, however, had been as enchanted with his intelligence and manners as Elinor knew she would be.

When the sisters were alone in Elinor's room that night, Joan gave her a sisterly kiss. "My dear, I'm so happy for both of you. I know you'll deal perfectly together. The wonderful thing about a happy marriage is that you love him totally now, but as the years go on, you will love him even more because your capacity to love grows." She settled herself on the bed near the pile of neatly stacked trousseau items.

"That doesn't seem possible." Elinor sighed and sat beside her sister. "I love him so much now I can hardly stand it." She flung her arms out to encompass her room.

"Yes, that's obvious with both of you going around smelling of April and May. But, Elinor, there are times when . . . well, when it seems as if your love isn't enough. So many times Michael has problems I can't help him cope with — hurts I can't heal." Joan ran her hand softly over a piece of delicately embroidered linen that Elinor had put away in her chest years ago.

"But what do you do? I feel as if I should

be able to put my arms around him and make it all right."

"I pray for Michael."

Elinor gaped. It sounded so simple. "And that helps?" Then she became defensive. "Well, I pray too. We use the prayer book in church." Did her sister think she was a heathen?

"No, dear, not from a book — from your heart. Just like I'm talking to you here. You see, love and marriage are not the answer to life's problems. God is the answer to the problems of life *and* marriage. I do wish you could return to Chatteris with me for a time. You could see what I'm talking about."

Elinor frowned thoughtfully, and Joan gave her time to assimilate the idea before going on. "Listen, Robert Hall is speaking in Cambridge this week. If you and Brandley will come with me, you'll see what I mean."

The Silbert party arrived at the St. Andrews Baptist meeting house in Cambridge on the final night of the four days of services. The renowned speaker had drawn an audience from all levels of the community. Men of the highest intellect and culture, leaders in the church, the bar, and the university, as well as shopkeepers, farmers, and servants had gathered to hear Robert Hall preach.

Just outside the door, Dr. Silbert was hailed by a fellow don in his flowing black academics and his wife in an equally flowing pelisse of puce satin. The couple obviously had taken great pains to learn the speaker's history.

Dr. Silbert hadn't yet closed his mouth after presenting his family to Dr. and Mrs. Ainsworth when the pedant announced, "We shall no doubt hear a remarkable homily. It is said that Mr. Hall taught himself the alphabet by the help of gravestones."

"*And* he wrote hymns before he was nine years old," Mrs. Ainsworth quickly added.

"As I was saying," the pedant continued, giving his spouse a quelling look, "I was informed that he was put up to preach at the age of eleven —"

Again Mrs. Ainsworth broke in. "And just think, the dear man has struggled all his life with a feeble constitution. What a cross he has had to bear with his physical infirmities. It puts one in mind of Saint Paul. And I know what it is to suffer. Why, only last week —"

Stepping in front of her, Dr. Ainsworth cleared his throat. "His scholarly achievements in Greek and Latin are remarkable. The brilliant Greek oration which he pronounced upon his graduation from the University of Aberdeen is said to have been the finest ever heard."

Mrs. Ainsworth was obviously not an adversary to be outdone by so simple a maneuver. "Why, he and a fellow student were so famous for reading Greek together that they were nicknamed Plato and Herodotus by their comrades."

"*I* told you that, my dear," the professor said under his breath. "I am persuaded you will want to know, Silbert, that he served as classical master in the Bristol Academy."

Mrs. Ainsworth, her puce satin shimmering in the light from the chapel door, stepped valiantly once more into the fray. "And his hearers are often so moved that many stand to their feet without any volition of their own." But the verbal duel ended in a stalemate as Dr. Silbert reminded them that it was time for the service.

They found seats in the quickly filling chapel — a simple wooden structure converted from a stable early in the previous century and unadorned by the carvings and stained glass to which Brandley was accustomed. The singing of several unfamiliar hymns left him even more uncomfortable, especially as he heard a note of fervor in some of the voices around him.

Brandley remained detached as he observed the minister enter — a plain, but forceful-looking man with ample forehead and large, brilliant eyes that compelled attention. He announced his text: "Love your neighbor as yourself." It was a single unadorned statement, delivered unemphatically, and yet its very simplicity was gripping. Brandley folded his arms across his chest and leaned back, taking care not to crush his stiffly starched shirt.

Deepening evening shades fell through the windows of the old chapel. The whole place seemed as if held in a great spell. Surprisingly, the Scripture reading was not from the New Testament, but from Isaiah's picture of Christ:

> Surely he hath borne our griefs, and carried our sorrows: yet we did esteem him stricken, smitten of God, and afflicted. But he was wounded for our transgressions, he was bruised for our iniquities: the chastisement of our peace was upon him; and with his stripes we are healed.

"The ultimate example of loving one's neighbor is Christ's love for each one of us as He hung on the cross."

Brandley shifted uneasily.

"How then are we to reach that high calling of the commandment? He who would obey Christ in this cannot love his neighbor without first rising higher still. He must love *himself* as God loves him.

"The man who will love his neighbor cannot do so by exercise of the will. It is the man fulfilled by God from whom he came and by whom he is, who alone can love his neighbor, who also came from God and is by God. In God alone can man meet himself as a person of value."

There was a solemn intensity, a breathless silence in the chapel. Brandley felt the speaker's eyes on him as Hall's rapid glance seemed to survey each face in the congregation. Almost as a reflex, Brandley shifted his position on the wooden bench.

"Only when a man loves God with all his heart will he love his neighbor as himself. There is no other goal of human perfection, no other object more central to the Father's will.

"And the great paradox is this — although you can't love your neighbor unless you love yourself and fully accept yourself as God has made you, this love of one's neighbor is the only door out of the dungeon of self. The man chained to self thinks mostly about himself. He thinks life is having, knowing, enjoying only himself; whereas, if he would forget himself, he would begin to enjoy a life of freedom in God and with his neighbors. Self is his dungeon."

The room seemed suffocating. It was becoming harder to concentrate. Why didn't someone open a window? Brandley glanced around, but no one else seemed ill at ease. What had Hall said about the dungeon of self? Elinor had called him Narcissus . . . Could self-hatred lead to self-absorption in an inverted way? On the surface it appeared to be a logical absurdity.

"One who looks only at himself rather than looking at God will be imprisoned as truly as one locked behind iron bars. Nay, the bondage will be worse, for imprisonment of the mind is far worse than imprisonment of the body.

"He who would be free must be freed by love. He must give love to God and his neighbor. This love will then be reflected back on him in ever greater fulfillment of the great circle of life."

The speaker leaned forward. As his rapid cadences filled the room, his very stature seemed to grow. Again Brandley shifted. He couldn't locate the source of his discomfort. The stuffy room? The ache in his hip? No physical explanation seemed adequate.

★ ★ ★

When the preacher first came to the pulpit, Elinor had been sorely disappointed by his thin, weak voice. He gestured little, only twitched his fingers nervously. His left hand rested palm downward on the lower part of his back where he suffered incessant pain. It seemed that because of his feeble voice, he had adopted a rapid pace to make up for what he lacked in fullness of tone. This method of delivery required both for himself and the audience an occasional pause, which emphasized each point and drove it home without interrupting the sweep of his words.

"God made you; you are not here by happenstance. You are here at this time and in the purposes of God to accomplish His will. As soon as you unite yourself to God by obedient action, the truth that is in Him becomes clear to you, shining from the wholeness of your new being in Christ."

No other sounds competed with the preacher's voice. Every eye was fixed upon him. Much to her surprise, Elinor found herself charmed and fascinated by Robert Hall's latent energy.

He seemed to gather momentum from the congregation. The power and sureness of his movements made every inflection dynamic. He reflected this vitality back upon those who were already alive to the inspiration. Excitement and tension permeated the air. The chapel itself held its breath.

"The commandment to love your neighbor is given four times in the Bible — but never without the command to love yourself." He distinctly formed each word, punctuating the final phrase with slow, soft blows of his firmly clenched fist on the scarred podium.

As the orator increased in animation, five or six of his hearers gripped the pews in front of them and rose to their feet, leaning forward, still keeping their eyes fixed on the speaker.

"Love is the core of all relationships, the only thing that brings true unity. But human love is not sufficient; it has to be God's love working in and through man."

Human love is not sufficient. Only days before Joan had said that very thing to Elinor. Was this the answer? Was there a whole new kind of love that she could experience and then give to Brandley in a healing way? She leaned forward in her seat.

Although others in the congregation came to their feet, grasping the backs of the seats in front of them, Elinor was hardly aware of the movement around her. She and Brandley might have been the only persons in the pews, for the preacher's words made her poignantly sensitive to the man sitting beside her. How was he responding to this? She ached to turn to him, but the intensity of the atmosphere held her focus on her own needs.

"As we live in love for our neighbors, we must also learn to let ourselves be loved. It is not enough that love is offered to us; we must receive it. God's love does not love that which is already worthy of being loved, but *creates* that which is worthy of His love.

"God *is* love. We love Him because He first loved us. God is *love*. Coming to God is responding to love. *God is love.*"

Elinor felt her thoughts and emotions drawn upward. She knew if she let go, she would come out of her seat. Her damp palms clenched her handbag.

"To know the love that God has for us will help us to have proper and real love for ourselves and then to give that love to others. This is the only possible way. Jesus Christ is the only one who accepts us as we are, the only one who can unchain us from the dungeon of self." The words came more slowly as if in awe of the very power of which they spoke.

Elinor sat very still, hardly breathing, her eyes closed. The ache of tenderness for her beloved beside her lost focus as her feelings centered on a new emotion — an awareness of need. She had not known before that such love as the preacher spoke of existed, had not known that anything was lacking in her life. This divine love that Hall described suddenly became an all-consuming desire, and she knew that she could never be happy or complete without it.

"Accept His love — open your heart to receive His love — trust His unfailing kindness — commit yourself to Him."

With a mental action as clear as the physical act of opening a door, Elinor opened her heart and gave a silent, ecstatic cry to God, *I love You.*

Immediately the ache and turmoil receded, replaced by a surge of peace and joy. Tears spilled from the corners of her eyes, and she knew with unmistakable certainty that everything would be all right. God had accepted her; He would fill her life with His love and His peace as Robert Hall had promised.

The preacher's final words were lost to Elinor in the blaze of her own release. Those of the congregation who had been brought to their feet reluctantly, slowly resumed their seats. The very building seemed to give a great sigh.

★ ★ ★

Everyone was moving, talking, smiling —
Brandley with them, but not a part of them.
Snatches of the sermon kept going over and
over in his head. *You cannot love someone else
unless you love yourself the way God made you.
. . . cannot love . . .*

Though outwardly calm, Brandley experienced an inner turbulence of self-interroga-
tion on the drive home. Did he really want
to let go? Even if he believed? Or like Byron's
prisoner of Chillon, had he and his chains
become friends? Did he want to be un-
chained from the dungeon of self, as Hall
styled it?

He knew better than to attempt to sleep,
so he went instead to his library. Somewhere
in all these books there had to be a Bible.
He was sure he remembered unpacking one.
He searched the shelves in the flickering light
of his candle. One large black volume on the
top shelf looked promising, but it turned out
to be a compilation of Greek philosophies.
He got down on his hands and knees to
search the lower shelves. He finally located
what he was looking for and extracted it
from between two volumes of Plato's *Repub-
lic*. After blowing the dust off, he sat for
some time with the Bible on his lap unopened.

It was unusual for Brandley to be at a loss with a book. But really just where would one start reading? He began with some unfruitful scouting in the Old Testament — Leviticus and Numbers didn't have much to say about love. The Psalms were beautiful, but not what he was looking for.

He decided to try the New Testament and found St. Paul talking about self-love in Ephesians. *So ought men to love their wives as their own bodies.* That was a good one, he thought bitterly. Then he sat for some time in a brown study before reading on. *He that loveth his wife loveth himself. . . . let every one of you in particular so love his wife even as himself.*

The words stunned him. He read them again, a frown between his brows, his mouth rigid. Was that what was lacking in his relationship with Elinor? Had he failed to love her or accept her love as fully as he should because he couldn't accept himself? If he was to love his wife as himself, he was going to have to get to work on himself. The uneasy suspicion that his problem was not physical, but spiritual, grew steadily until it was impossible to quell.

He got to his feet and began pacing the room. The idea was at war with all his training, and yet it was impossible to reject.

There was an authority to Robert Hall's words that would not be denied. Was it really possible that a personal God was so full of love for him that He could replace all his aversion for himself with a love that in turn could be given to Elinor? Though it was a magnetic idea, he doubted it.

16

A ray of light on the windowsill and the call of a bullfinch penetrated Brandley's consciousness as Molly bustled into the library with a cup of coffee. "Mester Brandley, what on earth dost tha' mean by sleeping on the sofa when tha's got a perfectly good bed of thy own upstairs? Doesn't tha' know much study is a weariness of the flesh?" She shook her head at his crumpled clothes and sunken eyes.

"Yes, I know. Your aunt often reminded me of the same thing." He took the coffee with a grave look. "But you don't know what I've been studying, Mrs. Hibbley." He took a sip of the steaming, strong coffee as he watched her eyes follow his gaze to the Bible that had fallen to the floor when he dozed off. She picked it up reverently and placed it on the edge of his desk. "Mr. Hall is quite as insistent as you are on the existence of a personal God." He meant to tease her, but he immediately regretted the words. *Now I've done it — let myself in for a sermon for sure*. He held his breath.

To his surprise, she just smiled quietly. "That there be, sir." She left the room.

As always his mind drifted to Elinor. What had she thought about last night? He must talk to her. He summoned Croydon.

The sharp features and hollow cheeks of the tall, thin valet gave no hint of his alarm at his master's disarray, but his pale blue eyes narrowed as he examined the deep creases in the blue superfine jacket that had been sent up from Weston's less than two weeks ago. Croydon bore the jacket before him in both hands. It was several minutes before he returned to shave his master.

For one of the few times in his life, Brandley failed on his first attempt to arrange his neck cloth and had to call for another. By the time Croydon returned with a pair of highly polished top boots, however, the second cloth lay in precise folds, and Brandley left for the Silberts.

Katy answered his knock and informed him that Elinor and Joan were just finishing breakfast. He declined the offer to join them. He wasn't hungry, and he wanted to see Elinor alone. He would wait for her in the garden.

Seating himself on the familiar bench, he surveyed the scene of so many milestones of their relationship. It was a dear place to both of them. Wattle kept the lawn scrupulously free of fallen leaves and was preparing the flower beds for the coming winter. The mid-morning sunshine in the branches of autumn gold leaves made the trees shine like the sun itself.

It was only a few minutes before Elinor came to him with a bright smile on her lips and love for him shining in her eyes. Was it only his imagination that she was even more lighthearted than usual? *I wonder if I'll ever get used to this?* he thought. Every time he saw her, her beauty was a surprise to him. He took both her hands and kissed them, first in the palms and then on her delicate wrists.

But oddly enough, her happiness only further depressed his spirits. Her joy served as a foil to his gloom and made him more aware than ever of the gulf between them.

The night before, Elinor had observed Brandley's preoccupation and had respected it with her silence during the drive home. She had wanted to tell him about her prayer and the immense joy and assurance she felt. But with all her family in the carriage, there had been no opportunity for private conversation. Now reticence overcame her. She sat quietly, waiting for him to begin. She looked at him questioningly.

He read her thoughts. "I want to know what *you* thought — that's why I'm here."

Elinor wanted to choose her words carefully — to say the right thing. But it all bubbled up in her and came pouring out at once. "Oh, Brandley, it was so perfect. God must have known just exactly — I mean, of course, He did. I knew my love wasn't enough at times. I could see it. And it hurt because I didn't know what to do. I know you love me too. But sometimes the love isn't quite enough. Joan said that's the way it is though. When Michael needs something she can't give him, she prays for him. I wanted so much to be able to do that for you, Brandley; so that's why I prayed as Robert Hall directed us to last night. Well, not the only reason. I wanted His love in my own life. I need it too. And it's wonderful! Brandley, I'm so happy! It's that peace I was telling you about. The peace that's so different in Joan. Now I've found it too!" She stopped for breath and then filled the garden with her lovely laughter. "Oh dear, you didn't know what a chatterbox you were getting, did you?"

Her happiness reached out to him. But Brandley pulled back from it as a wounded animal would run from one who would aid it. "But I don't understand. You always were happy, the most contented person I've ever known."

"Yes, I was happy, especially since I found you." She smiled at him, almost shy again. "But now I guess my capacity for happiness has increased. Joan said something like that. She said our love and happiness would grow as we live and share together. She even invited me to Chatteris so I could see it with her and Michael. Isn't it all too wonderful!" She wanted to fling her arms out and embrace the world.

The radiance of her joy accentuated his own darkness. He spoke slowly, his solemnity increasing. "So you realized that too, did you? That as wonderful as our love is, it wasn't quite — didn't quite do everything?" He turned to her and grasped both her hands. "Robert Hall said you couldn't really love another person until you loved yourself. You deserve the best of everything. Especially love. I'm not sure I'm capable of that." He rose abruptly and stood with his back to her.

She nodded. The bubbles were gone now. "I know. I kept thinking that because your limp didn't bother me, pretty soon it wouldn't bother you either. But it hasn't worked that way." She looked up at him, her intensity giving emphasis to each word.

"I've wanted to say, 'Look, Brandley, you've got this all out of proportion. You limp. That's all. I'm sure it's inconvenient and uncomfortable, but why can't you get your mind off it?' But last night helped me to see it in a different light. It's not a matter of determination."

"The more perfect I've found you, my dear, the more I've loathed myself for being imperfect."

Elinor heard the agony in his voice. She slipped her hand into his.

Brandley stirred with the same mounting restlessness he had experienced at the meeting last night. Together they walked aimlessly for a few minutes. Because he had had so little sleep, the drag to his step was more pronounced than usual, but they were unaware of that right now.

Elinor searched for something to break the tension and oppressive mood. "I haven't seen Papa this morning. Let's go find out what he thought of our remarkable ecclesiastic." Brandley nodded in relief at finding a distraction for his own uncomfortable soul-searching.

They found the don at work in the library. As always he was perfectly willing to have his work interrupted by his family.

"It is said Hall's eloquence recommends

evangelical religion to persons of taste. I find that he has had a great influence on my mind." Dr. Silbert drew on his clay pipe thoughtfully. "I was most struck with the exquisite beauty and balance of his sentences. His words displayed, in an eminent degree, a rare excellence of conception and expression of thought, even delivered so rapidly."

Elinor wanted to cry out in protest against such an impersonal analysis of words that had been life-changing to her, but she sensed that Brandley needed the distance of a clinical approach. She laughed. "Oh, Papa, you're talking like a professor!"

"I'm afraid I can't help that, Princess. But I have been giving this considerable thought. After all, we have just heard the undisputed finest of all the dissenting preachers of our day." He emphasized his words by jabbing the air with his pipe stem. "It seemed to me that there was not the slightest semblance of parade, nothing that betrayed the least effort to be eloquent. But there was a power of thought, a grace of beauty, and yet force of expression. He commands the best language apparently without thinking of the language at all."

"Did you notice how his face seemed to glow from a fire within? I thought it was irresistible." Elinor could at least hint at what the experience had meant to her. "I have heard that Mr. Coleridge admits he is envious of Mr. Hall's perfect style, proclaiming it the best in the English language."

"High praise indeed," the professor agreed. His pipe had gone out; he laid it aside. "But I fancy him more in the mold of Dr. Johnson than of your romantic poet — if it were possible to conceive of Johnson as a dissenter, that is. I sense in Hall something of the lexicographer's mixture of pride and humility, of domination and self-abasement. Too, he has Johnson's love of common sense and homespun philosophy. I do believe, however, our speaker's imagination is more excursive than Johnson's." Dr. Silbert rested his elbows on the arms of his chair and tapped his widespread fingertips together thoughtfully.

"Like Johnson? No, I think not, sir. A modern Demosthenes is more like it — with perhaps a superior mind and greater elevation of sentiment even. I found him majestic without pretension and sensible without dullness. One of the great men of our day, I believe." Brandley looked surprised at his own lavish praise.

Elinor still longed to bring the conversation back to the content of Hall's sermon, not merely its delivery. "But didn't you feel that he spoke for his Master and not for himself?"

She got no further. Mustard burst into the room in her usual whirlwind manner. She had been in the kitchen with Katy and was unaware of her idol's arrival. She streaked into the room and planted herself at Brandley's feet with an expectant bark. Then she began sniffing and jumping, hunting for her piece of biscuit. After a moment's teasing, the biscuit was produced. Mustard accepted the morsel, laid it aside, and began licking Brandley's fingers in gratitude.

While intellectually stimulating, the discussion of Mr. Hall's style had not done much for Brandley's agitation. Elinor and Mustard accompanied him in thoughtful silence to his horse, brought forward by the attentive Cobbett. Brandley took Emrys's reins. He and Elinor looked at each other and smiled. She gave him her hand to kiss.

Brandley spent the rest of the afternoon in his library, even shutting out the faithful Page. No matter how he struggled against it, the conviction of what must be done grew in his mind. He wasn't sure when the seed had been planted, perhaps with his reading from St. Paul last night, but it had been fed and watered by his time with Elinor — her happiness, her words. On reflection he realized that even when speaking to her of their love, he had used the past tense. The pestilent plant was quickly growing to maturity, its tentacles grasping every part of his mind and reaching down to seize hold of his heart.

The horror of the act gripped him. Yet going on as things now stood was unthinkable. Present pain for both of them would be far better than a lifetime of unhappiness. Elinor herself had said their love wasn't enough. He had always known it while pushing the awareness to the back of his mind and focusing instead only on the good things. But it simply wouldn't do.

As evening shadows filled the room, Brandley sat with his head in his hands, his shoulders slumped. Finally, he raised his head with a sigh that came from the depths of his being, his features set in stony determination. "The deed is best done quickly." He dragged himself to his feet.

The road to the Silberts' home had never seemed so long. His mind remained frozen in inflexible resolution. The turmoil was stilled, replaced by an awful void.

"Send Elinor to me in the garden, if you please." His words rang with a cold formality that left Katy standing slack-jawed and blinking for several moments before she turned to do his bidding.

The news of her beloved's unexpected summons surprised Elinor. She quickly checked her appearance in the parlor mirror, tossed a soft shawl over her shoulders against the evening chill, and went out to him.

As her light step hurried down the garden path, Brandley turned to face her. At the sight of his forbidding countenance, she stopped short.

"Good evening." He made a stiff little bow.

"Brandley, what —" She took a hesitant step toward him.

"It is my most unpleasant task, my very painful task, to inform you that I find it necessary to cry off our betrothal. I have decided to accept the offer made to me some time ago of a university fellowship. As you are undoubtedly aware, university rules preclude the possibility of a fellow marrying.

"I will, of course, expect you to put it out that you cast me off as I'm sure that there can be little surprise among our acquaintances on that score. It is fortunate that the announcement of our engagement has not yet appeared in *The Gazette*, so there will be no need of a public notice.

"I would suggest that you consider accepting your sister's invitation to accompany her to Chatteris for an extended visit. That will give time for the nine days' wonder to wear off among the gossip mongers and save you undue embarrassment."

They stood facing each other in silence as if an invisible wall had dropped between them. Elinor's first impulse was to rush at that wall screaming and hitting it with both fists until it smashed to pieces. But she was held immobile by an icy hand squeezing her throat.

At long last she spoke, her words coming as from a long distance and sounding strange to her ears. "Is that what you want?"

His voice was harsh. "It will suit me much better."

She said nothing because she could think of nothing to say. She couldn't even take in the sense of Brandley's words. She felt as if she were sinking in a bad dream. An eternity passed before she was able to speak. "I see."

"We have shared a delightful companionship, but unwisely allowed our emotions to rule our heads — an unforgivable state of affairs for a classicist, I fear."

The only movement she made was to moisten her lips with her tongue. "I see."

"Whatever inconvenience and pain must

be attached to this circumstance will pass. You will soon be thanking God to be well out of an entanglement that could only have led to a lifetime of unhappiness."

Elinor blinked blindly. "I see." She choked the words past the constriction in her throat. But she didn't see anything. Blackness was closing in from every side. And the sightlessness of her eyes prevented her from seeing the desolation in his.

The latch on the garden gate snapped shut. She forced her way through the black horror of the nightmare back to the house refusing the solace of tears. Only the stricken look in her eyes betrayed her anguish.

She had one thing to cling to — only one, but it was enough. In her new relationship with Christ, she could feel His love when she couldn't feel Brandley's.

At noon on Tuesday the mail coach would depart from The Sun for Chatteris. She would be on it.

17

Molly heard the door slam. Alarmed by such an unaccustomed sound in Sir Hilliard's well-run establishment, she bustled in to discover the reason.

"Oh, Mester Brandley, sir. Tha' gave me quite a start. I've been worrying over dinner, but I'll warrant tha'll like it well enou."

"No dinner, Mrs. Hibbley. Send Croydon to me in the library."

But the baronet's orders were too much even for Croydon's well-schooled impassivity. "*Brandy*, sir?" Both eyebrows disappeared into his hairline. The baronet was not a teetotaler, but Croydon had never known him to indulge in spirits while alone.

"You heard me," Brandley snapped. "There must be some about the place — in the medicine chest or kitchen. Or send Barrow to The Sun to purchase some. Well, move, man! Don't stand here gaping as if I'd asked for live toads and arsenic!"

"Yes, sir. I mean, no, sir. Er, right away, sir." Croydon backed out of the room.

In a short time, his eyebrows held rigidly in their proper place, the valet reappeared bearing a bottle and snifter on a silver tray.

"Do you wish me to pour for you, sir?"

"No. I plan to sit and look at it all night," Brandley growled. "Of course, I want you to pour out!" Croydon splashed a little in the glass. "A full glass!" Croydon poured, then hovered uncertainly. "You may leave the bottle." Brandley ran his hand roughly through his dark locks. "I intend to do a thoroughly unscholarly thing and get shockingly castaway."

"Yes, sir." Croydon nodded his head. "Will that be all, sir?"

"You had best send to Trinity to find out what Hollis concocts for Verdun after one of his rounders. I intend to have need of it."

"Very good, sir."

"No, it is not very good. It is abominable. But it is done."

But even as the liquor numbed Brandley's brain and blurred his sight, it could not remove his sense of loss. As he became less aware of his surroundings, the vision that he had been able to push into his subconscious when in firmer control engulfed him. He had seen Elinor's pain. Her eyes loomed before him, haunting him with their own haunted look.

His thoughts became increasingly maudlin as the ominous abyss of the future yawned before him. With one fell stroke he had destroyed all the happiness he had ever possessed — happiness far beyond anything he had ever dreamed possible. He had been right — it *was* impossible. And as *The Clouds* prophesied, Zeus had sent a rain of remorse dashing against his perjury and left him to repent. He raised his glass in salute to *The Clouds* and drank it to the bottom.

On his third refill his hand shook, spilling a small pool of the pale amber liquid onto the silver tray. A few sips and his charred brain knew it had had enough. If he didn't go to bed now, he wouldn't get there. A fuzzy idea of summoning Croydon occurred to him, but, of course, he could make it himself. He wasn't really foxed.

Unsteadily, he hauled himself from his sprawled position in his chair near the fireplace. He stood for a moment gripping the edge of the side table. Attempting a step, he lost his balance. He fell heavily on his weak left side, crashing against the massive oak desk in the center of the room. The shock of excruciating pain sobered his senses. Gripping the edge of the desk for support, he snatched the liquor bottle from the table by his chair and hurled it against the stone fireplace, sending broken glass and the remaining contents of the bottle over the carpet and the wall.

As the pain took a firmer grip on him, he knew the momentary fear that by his stupid action he might have turned himself into an out-and-out cripple. He uttered an oath. Then the pain overcame him. He sank to the floor.

The acrid smell of burning feathers assailed Brandley's nostrils and made him choke. "Take those blasted things away." He fanned the air with his hand. "Help me get up. And close those dashed curtains." He blinked bloodshot eyes at the early morning sun streaming in the library windows. Croydon unceremoniously half carried, half dragged his master to the upholstered chair by the fireplace. Then he departed and returned in a moment bearing a tankard which he presented with perfect aplomb.

"And what is that vile stuff?" Brandley demanded.

"It is Mr. Verdun's recipe, sir. You asked for it."

"Oh, yes, I seem to remember something of the sort. Very well." Brandley gulped the potion down, grimacing at its bitterness. "That's bad enough to make a teetotaler of a publican." He thrust the mug at his man-servant.

"Shall I send for a doctor, sir?"

"What? Because I got foxed? Oh, the hip." He grimaced as he allowed momentary awareness of the incessant pain he had stoically refused to admit. He dropped one hand into the other. "Yes, I suppose you'd better."

Croydon left, and Molly entered with a dustpan and broom to clear away the traces of the night's debauch.

"Well, Molly, your aunt would now subject me to a thorough scolding. Don't you consider that your prerogative too?"

She considered him for a moment and then shook her head. "I can't think tha'll be needin' it, sir."

A bitter, self-mocking laugh escaped him. "How right you are, Mrs. Hibbley. No one could possibly be harder on me than I'm being on myself — fool that I am."

He sat dismally while Molly cleaned up the scattered bits of broken glass. She swept and brushed and polished, carefully moving every accessory, even those far out of range of the shattered bottle. At last Brandley became aware of the unaccustomed deliberateness of her motions.

"All right, Molly, let's have it. I can see you've something on your mind."

"Well, yes, that I have, sir. I was just a'thinking the thing tha' should do when tha's able is go on over to King's College and have a chat with Mester Simeon about whatever it is that's a worrying tha'."

"Simeon? Well, thank you for your advice, Mrs. Hibbley. We shall see."

Molly exited with her broom and dustpan. In order to keep at bay his old dread of being pulled about by a physician, Brandley turned his thoughts to the first time he had heard of Simeon. He had been with a group of about fifty undergraduates during his first weeks at Cambridge. Someone had asked whom the gownsmen would turn to for counsel in trouble, and on a ballot nearly all named Simeon. Brandley had not taken part in the balloting since he knew so few people at the university yet. Then he heard Simeon deliver the college sermon last June. And now it seemed the name was forever being flung at him by his housekeeper.

The door opened, and Croydon entered with Dr. Marston. The fat doctor was loud and hearty, rushing in like a gust of wind, dispensing cheerful trivialities that made Brandley grit his teeth more than the pain did.

"What have we here now?" He probed at the injured side. "Well, you did do a thorough job of it, didn't you? No fever though, so I don't suppose it will be necessary to bleed you." He sounded almost disappointed.

The examination was as uncomfortable as Brandley had foreseen, but the doctor's pronouncement not so gloomy as he feared.

"Yes, a severe blow, I see, very severe. How did it come about? Been sporting the fives?"

Brandley glared at him.

"Ah, well." The doctor cleared his throat. "The thing now is that you give it as much time to heal as possible. Stay entirely off your feet for a few days, nice excuse for a lay-up. Then use a walking stick thereafter until you've got your strength back."

"A stick!" Brandley groaned at the humiliation.

"It is *most* important, sir." The doctor was firm.

Brandley rang the bell on the table at his elbow, and Molly bustled in. "See that Dr. Marston has some refreshment, Mrs. Hibbley. He is leaving now."

Molly returned shortly. It was apparent that the good doctor had had a word with her, for she set about her task of making the master comfortable on the sofa. Croydon entered on her heels, bearing the master's dressing gown.

"There now. Tha'll be as comfortable as

281

tha' can, Mester Brandley." Molly gave the cushions a final plump.

. "I shall be as comfortable as I deserve to be," Brandley growled.

"Would you like some laudanum drops now, sir?" Croydon inquired.

"Certainly not! Just go and leave me in peace."

His domestics departed, leaving Brandley in quiet, if not in peace. He hadn't been sofa-bound since he was thirteen. But all the aversion he felt to the restriction as a youth returned in force, and internally he chaffed like a fretful child. From long practice he could ignore the pain, but submitting to inactivity required greater fortitude. He soon found concentrating on his research to be more effort than it was worth, so he was left with time to think. But that was depressing. His brain was a muddle of thoughts of Elinor and of Robert Hall's sermon.

Molly interrupted his disconsolate reflections by ushering in Charlie.

"I say, you look thoroughly knocked about," his friend greeted him cheerfully.

Brandley gave him a fierce look. "I shall live."

"Saw Elinor at The Sun. Said she was going home with her sister. What kind of a hum is this?"

"It's no hum," Brandley assured him in an acid voice. "Cried off."

"Can't cry off. Not at all the thing. Very bad ton." Charlie frowned. "Who cried off?"

"It is always the lady who cries off."

Charlie scrutinized him. "Cutting a wheedle. Must be." When Brandley didn't answer, he sighed. "Ramshackle business. Anything I can do?"

Brandley declined the offer, and Charlie soon left shaking his head over what a muddle someone with a double first class could make of things.

It was several hours later before Brandley received another visitor. Molly, with flushed cheeks and overly bright eyes that betrayed her excitement and nervousness, ushered in a sharp-featured man of middling height with flashing eyes and receding gray hair. He was meticulously dressed in a short black coat, breeches, and gaiters with a white ruffled shirt under his flowing black academics that hung well back on his shoulders.

"Mester Charles Simeon, sir," Molly announced and then disappeared.

"Forgive my not rising, sir." Brandley's good manners covered his surprise at this unexpected intrusion. "I am a bit, ah, indisposed. Please be seated."

His eyes twinkling and a small smile playing around his lips, Simeon gave a formal bow and took a chair near the sofa.

"Am I right in inferring that our good Mrs. Hibbley has sprung my presence on you as a surprise?"

Brandley gave a small laugh. "A bit like that, sir. Although she has made no secret of her belief that we should meet."

Simeon nodded in agreement. "So she has assured me. A very determined woman, your Mrs. Hibbley."

At that moment the determined Mrs. Hibbley entered the room bearing a tea tray laden with cakes, biscuits, and a large plate of flat hot oatcakes, which she presented with pride.

"Why, Molly, fresh bannocks! You have quite outdone yourself." Brandley took one and spread it thickly with fresh, sweet butter. "A Yorkshire specialty," he explained to his guest.

"Tha'll like them graidely, Mester Reverend, sir," Molly assured him.

"I'm sure I shall, Mrs. Hibbley. I'm sure I shall." Simeon smiled broadly. His fondness for the table was well known.

Having done all she could to further the cause, Molly left the men alone. They chatted for a time about Simeon's famous homiletical outlines, to which he was now writing an appendix. Even such a thoroughly secular student as Brandley had heard of this series of discourses which formed a commentary on every book of the Old and New Testament.

"Slowly. It is progressing very slowly," Simeon said between sips of tea. "When I completed the eleventh volume of the *Homileticae*, I thought I had done with it. But now I fear the appendix may extend to six volumes. But I daresay, as an author yourself, you understand how it is."

With this adroit turn, he led Brandley to talk of his own work, and from there the conversation moved to Brandley telling his listener of the hollowness of this long-sought achievement. Unrest, dissatisfaction, skepticism — somehow they all found their way into the conversation.

Simeon nodded understandingly and then set his cup aside. "You know, I was only a few years younger than yourself when I came to face those same issues. Not easy ones, are they?"

Brandley shook his head. Simeon continued, "My first religious impressions began while I was at Eaton — the American War Fast Day in 1776, it was. The idea of a whole nation uniting to repent, fast, and pray made me think. Then on going up to

Cambridge in 1779, I found that attendance at Holy Communion was required. I didn't think much about it at first, but gradually I became aware of my unfitness to take the sacrament. I began to look to my spiritual life much as I suspect you have done."

Brandley's nod was almost imperceptible.

"I began by reading Venn's *Whole Duty of Man*."

Brandley smiled wryly, thinking of sitting in early chapel, the curate's droning words bouncing off his glazed inattention.

Simeon saw the smile. "No, it didn't help me much either, except to stimulate my anxiety. Then I joined the Society for the Promotion of Christian Knowledge. For about three anxious months, I tried everything I could find to live a Christian life, but none of it really answered. Then one night while reading a sermon by Bishop Wilson on the Lord's Supper, I was led to put my whole trust in Christ rather than in my own worth. Meeting Him put my entire life into perspective."

"And you've never doubted since, sir?" Brandley frowned skeptically and leaned back on the sofa.

"My dear fellow, how I wish I could tell you that." The older man smiled, but he shook his head wistfully. "I must confess that my habits of faith and devotion were at first interrupted by a lapse as serious as drunkenness. But my faith grew, and it has remained with me through life."

Brandley leaned forward again. He found this confession from such a holy man astounding. His religious experience must have been valid to have resulted in such a change.

They talked for some time, Simeon giving patient and learned answers to Brandley's skeptical questions. When Simeon rose to take his leave, Brandley's mind was whirling. Yet there seemed to be a spot of tranquility at the center. Perhaps he was on the right path.

Before bidding his host a warm farewell, Simeon searched the folds of his academical and extracted two volumes. "Here. This is the book that set me on the right path." He handed Brandley Bishop Wilson's work and then a volume of sermons by Martin Luther. "And this is the sermon that set John Wesley in the right way when he heard it preached in Aldersgate Chapel."

"Yes, I've heard of that. Felt his heart 'strangely warmed,' I believe he said."

"That's right. You see, until that time he had been trusting in himself to earn his own peace by good works, and no one could do more good works than Wesley. Up at four o'clock every morning for two hours of prayer, then an hour of Bible reading before going to jails, prisons, and hospitals to minister until late at night. Did this for ten years without finding peace; even went to the American Colonies as a missionary. A storm at sea on his return made him realize that he had no assurance he would go to Heaven if he died. When he came back and heard this sermon, he realized that saving faith was trusting in Christ alone — not in his own works."

Simeon was almost to the door where Molly stood quietly to show him out when he added, "And when you're up and about, you just pop over some Friday evening for one of our little conversation parties. We have them every week during the school year. Very informal, you know — just a nice cup of tea and good fellowship. Six o'clock."

Before the outside door clicked shut, Brandley was reading. Happy to have found a focus for his disordered thoughts, he gave the volumes his full concentration.

He was still reading two hours later when Molly brought his dinner on a tray. "Molly, I am most indebted to you for your meddling. Rev. Simeon was an invigorating visitor."

Molly gave him an I-told-you-so look and went about setting out his dinner on a small table near the sofa.

The remainder of the week crept by. The only good news Brandley received was a letter from the University Press informing him that his book would be released in two weeks. The work would be formally presented to the university community at a reception in the author's honor, to which all university dons would be invited.

Friday morning Dr. Marston called on his patient. In his irritatingly bracing manner, he informed Brandley that he was now free to walk as long as he used a stick. Croydon appeared on the heels of the doctor's departure with a sturdy, no-nonsense implement, unlike those affected by some gentlemen of fashion to complete their wardrobes.

"Where did you get that awful thing, Croydon?" Brandley demanded.

"From the apothecary, sir. Dr. Marston said —"

"Oh, dash it all, never mind what the doctor said. Let's have it."

So it was that two days later, Brandley, leaning heavily on the despised stick, handed his phaeton over to a groom at King's and made his way to the stately Gibbs Building where Charles Simeon had rooms on the top floor. There were four flights of steep, dark stairs to be climbed, the right foot always first. Outside the door Brandley noted several substantial shoe-scrapers. And from the look of the floor, he was not the first to arrive. The many capes on the row of pegs above the scrapers confirmed this.

Rev. Simeon met him at the door and shook his hand, smiling and bowing with the grace of a courtier. This was his manner of greeting all his guests, but none could have appreciated it more than this newcomer who had not entirely conquered his dread of meeting strangers. The spacious room into which he was ushered was filled with rows of benches, most of them already occupied.

Even crowded as it was, Brandley could see that the suite was magnificent. Simeon's writing desk stood in front of a large arched window looking out over a green expanse of lawn spilling down to the river where a gentle curtain of willows and stately elms rose to the skyline.

Brandley accepted a cup of tea, which one of the servants poured from a black Wedgwood teapot, and settled somewhat uncomfortably on a bench near the fireplace. Sipping his tea, he observed the assembly. Sitting in small groups, they were talking animatedly. Most were regular attendants at these parties, and each arrival was hailed by a group of friends, which he joined. This was the first levee since the long vacation, and old friends heartily greeted one another, introducing classmates brought with them for the first time. Few students would refuse an invitation to attend a Simeon conversation party — at least once. But only the serious-minded would become regulars. As Brandley surveyed the lively conversation groups, he felt distinctly isolated.

The room continued to fill. Sixty or seventy gownsmen squeezed into the room, and the host greeted each newcomer in his old-fashioned, gentlemanly manner. As a guest was introduced to him, Simeon would produce a memorandum book and enter the name of his new acquaintance.

Finally Rev. Simeon took his elevated seat by the fireplace. He sat with his hands folded upon his knees, his head turned a little to one side, the sharp-featured visage solemn and composed. After a pause, he began to speak in a slow, soft voice. "Now if you have any questions to ask, I shall be happy to hear them and to give what assistance I can."

Immediately the air filled with questions, mostly from divinity students. Many went beyond Brandley's theological knowledge. But when one questioner asked Mr. Simeon about his struggle in overcoming guilt, Brandley's attention again awakened.

"Yes, indeed, a severe struggle, my friend. I spent hours trying to reconcile my sense of guilt with the mystery of the sacrifice of Christ. Then on the Tuesday of Holy Week of 1779, I came upon a phrase to the effect that 'the Jews knew what they did when they transferred their sin to the head of their offering.' Like a flash it came to me — I can transfer all my guilt to Another! I sought to lay my sins upon the sacred head of Jesus.

"On Wednesday I began to have a hope of mercy; on Thursday that hope increased; on Friday and Saturday it became more strong; and on Sunday morning — Easter Day — I awoke early with the words upon my heart and lips, 'Jesus Christ is risen today! Hallelujah! Hallelujah!' " The excitement of his voice rose with his words. Everyone in the room, including Brandley, sensed the immensity of the experience. "From that hour peace flowed in rich abundance in my soul." The room was quiet.

Brandley looked around him and could find no spot to set his cup where it would not be in danger of being stepped on. The room was stifling, and his crowded seat on the hard, narrow bench was making his hip ache.

The conversation moved on to the area of recreation. Simeon told the assembled gownsmen that God's creation existed for man's enjoyment.

"Don't be afraid of God's blessings or reject them like monks, but serve God in your recreations and *enjoy Him*. Our rule should be to enjoy God in everything — to feel the delight of affluence, science, friends, recreation, children, in fact, of everything as coming to us from God." Simeon was known for his exuberant horsemanship and indefatigable walking.

Brandley liked that. He had no fondness for Cromwellian Puritanism and had wondered if these evangelicals also might require long-faced asceticism.

"There are but two lessons for the Christian to learn. The one is to enjoy God in everything; the other is to enjoy everything in God."

It was late when the party broke up. The stars shone around a slim new moon as Brandley drove home. The only sound was the clop of his horse's hooves on cobblestones. After the stuffy room, the sharp cold air felt wonderful.

All the way home Brandley meditated on Simeon's parting admonition: "Determine to know nothing among you save Jesus Christ and Him crucified."

18

Ten days later Elinor returned to Cambridge. Her invitation from Joan had been open-ended, and her sister pressed her to stay. "At least a month, dear. You're wonderful company for me and such a help. I really don't know what I shall do when you leave."

"Gammon!" Elinor laughed, although the humor didn't reach her eyes. "As if you hadn't been coping exceedingly well without me for years. I can see perfectly well that you don't think me convalescent yet — not well enough to tread so near the ogre's den."

"Elinor, I —"

"Silly, don't look like that! I appreciate your concern, and I've loved being here with the children and making parish calls with you and all. It has helped. Truly it has. But I can't stay hidden for the rest of my life. Cambridge is my home. The sooner I go back and pick up the pieces of my life, the better it will be. You know it's much easier to repair a seam before it has time to fray."

Her brave words sounded hollow in her own ears. She had spoken more for her own benefit than for Joan's. It had to be faced, so why not now? The idea of staying away until she ceased to care was idiocy. She knew she would always care. Now at least she had the comfort and assurance of knowing that she wasn't alone. In just this brief time, she had grown closer yet to God, and daily, even hourly, she experienced the great love He offered.

On her second day home, however, she began to wonder whether she had been courageous or foolhardy in returning. A mounting restlessness made it impossible to settle to reading or sewing. Mrs. Silbert pressed her daughter to accompany her on some social calls; but Elinor, knowing that veiled allusions to "that awkward situation" would be more than she could bear, adamantly refused.

Instead, she asked Cobbett to saddle Pallas for her. The autumn weather would not hold much longer. Indeed, several days of rain the past week had warned of winter's approach. But as today was crisp and sunny, she would ride.

Without thinking, she directed Pallas to her favorite ride on the fen. A short time later she became aware of the course she was taking. She pulled up sharply and started to turn, but then she stopped. No, it was better to go on. Running away hadn't helped. Per-haps facing the pain directly would exorcise the ghost. The very spot where she and Brandley had met was burned into her mem-ory. Even if her mother and she hadn't re-turned to paint the landscape, she would not have forgotten.

But no two scenes could be more unlike. The tender green of the spring grass had turned to a coarse, drab olive. The trees, whose lacy boughs had called forth such de-lightful allusions to Daphne and Apollo, were now stripped stark and bare to stand unprotected against the wintery blasts. Eli-nor shuddered and turned her face away, unshed tears stinging her eyes.

She had cried only once. Her first night at Joan's she had released her tenacious grip on her emotions and allowed the tears to flood her pillow, hoping they would wash away the hurt. They didn't, but the release was probably good for her. Joan had tactfully stayed away until the tears were replaced by dry, racking sobs and had then gone in to hold her sister in her arms.

So nothing was to be gained by a repeat. She was determined to look forward, not backward. In time, she told herself, she would learn to live with being crippled on the inside just as Brandley had learned to live with being crippled on the outside. And she had one consolation, one thing that could never be taken from her — she could always pray for him.

Suddenly Pallas's ears pricked forward. Elinor froze, afraid to breathe. She strained her ears, then blinked, as if that would sharpen her hearing. There was no mistaking. She did hear hoofbeats. They were coming louder and louder and were just around the bend.

"Elinor!" The rider checked his horse sharply.

She turned to face him, trying not to show her disappointment. "Hello, Charlie."

"Surprise to find you here. Thought you were in Chatteris."

"I came back."

"I can see that." It was unlike easygoing Charlie to be in nervous fidgets. He looked at his hands, stroked his horse's neck, tugged at his collar, and cleared his throat.

Finally she took pity on him and changed the subject. "What brings you here?"

"Been to Madingley. Miss Underhill promised to accompany me to the reception for Hil— , ah, er . . ." He turned red and looked in danger of spurring his horse away in mad flight.

Elinor shook her head. "It's all right,

Charlie. It is idiotic to think I'm such a peagoose that I can't bear to hear his name spoken. How is Sir Brandley?"

Elinor's openness caused Charlie to relax. "Ain't at all the thing."

"But he must be excited about his fellowship. Will he keep his residence or move into university rooms?" To her surprise, she found talking about Brandley an excellent balm. She suddenly realized she hadn't heard his name spoken aloud for three weeks. These were questions she had longed to ask her parents, but she had been afraid of giving them pain.

Charlie frowned at her in confusion. "You gone queer in the attic? Hilliard's not become a fellow. Not moving either. Not very far. On the sofa for a week. Still has a stick."

All the blood drained from Elinor's face. She felt lightheaded, and for a moment she feared she might faint. "He's been ill?" Her voice was barely above a whisper.

"Oh, no. Shot the cat. Bad fall. Served him right. Told him it wasn't at all the thing. Shouldn't have cried off. Ramshackle business. Told him."

"Charlie! Stop it this instant! Are you telling me that Brandley did *not* accept a fellowship, but instead went on some kind of a — a bacchanal and injured himself?"

"Been telling you so."

"Oh, that stupid, bacon-brained . . . oh
. . ." She kicked Pallas sharply and reined
her for home, leaving Charlie in the middle
of the road shaking his head.

The morning of the University Press reception, Brandley found his spirits unexpect-
edly high. He had given the whole affair little
thought previously, but now that it was but
a few hours away, the excitement of seeing
his long-awaited work, of actually holding
the volume in his hands, had hit him.

He put his quill down with a sigh and ran
a hand impatiently through his hair.
Simeon's books lay before him on the desk.
During the past days they had been read,
laid aside, and read again. Now would be as
good a time as any to return them.

So once more Brandley haltingly climbed
the stairs of the Gibbs Building, but this time
not leaning on his stick so heavily as before.
Mr. Simeon's personal servant opened the
door and ushered Brandley into the spacious
apartment. No longer crowded with benches
and gownsmen, its graceful proportions were
apparent. Simeon was seated at his writing
desk, but he quickly removed his spectacles,
put his work aside, and assured the servant
that he would be only too happy to take time

to meet with his friend.

"I'm sorry to disturb you," Brandley apologized.

"Oh, no! What! Are we to sleep? Why if I were to call upon you in your rooms, I should not find you asleep, should I? No, we must work while it is called today."

Much amused by this reception, Brandley sat on a small sofa near Simeon's desk. Simeon folded his hands on top of his desk and got right to the heart of the matter. "Have you found what you're looking for yet?"

Simeon patiently answered Brandley's numerous questions from his reading of Luther and Wilson, checking off a precise list in his mind as they progressed. When the list appeared to be finished, Simeon said, "My son, you're working too hard. Although intellectual understanding and change of will are closely related, faith isn't a mathematical examination to be passed. It is, rather, accepting love. Accepting it in simple faith, not by any preset mechanism or formula. Love should be the spring of all actions. The proper model of our love for each other is Christ's love to us."

Brandley was quiet, relating these words to Hall's, as Simeon continued. "There is another thing which I would suggest —

namely that you are too much occupied in looking at yourself and too little in beholding the Lord Jesus Christ. It is by the former that you are to be humbled; but it is by the latter that you are to be changed into the divine image."

Brandley stared. How could he know? Had Molly told him? Or was Simeon reading his mind?

Simeon knew full well the area most likely to be a stumbling block to the classical scholar. "Your learning must not be set in competition with the Word of God, but must be made subservient to it. Reason, in those things that are within its sphere, is a useful though not an infallible guide. And, in the things that are beyond its sphere, it has its office; it ceases to be a guide, indeed, but it becomes a companion. Though revealed religion is neither founded on human reason nor makes its appeal to it, yet it is perfectly consistent with it."

Brandley nodded slowly, thoughtfully, as Simeon continued, "The Bible provides answers on the fundamental issues of life for which there are no purely academic answers."

Brandley felt within himself an openness to Simeon's counsel. The tension and struggle he had felt at Robert Hall's service were gone. He was listening willingly.

But then Simeon's servant opened the door. Apologizing profusely, Simeon's curate entered the room requesting a conference with his master on a matter of pressing importance. The learned counselor rose with a nod. "I trust you will pardon me, Sir Brandley." Simeon went out, closing the door.

Brandley sat in silence for several moments. Then as he meditated, he began to feel as if a door were opening inside him, shedding light in a darkened chamber, a light that drove the dark, soul-stifling clouds from his mind and replaced them with a Living Being.

He spoke aloud to the empty room. "Yes." He said it slowly. Then he spoke with conviction. "I believe."

Something inside him that had been overstretched and held at the breaking point for a long time slowly unwound. As the tension drained away from the recesses of his soul, his fetters let loose. The chains fell off, and a peace and lightness he had never known took its place. Quietly the peace he had sought and thought never to find engulfed him. Brandley's search had ended.

The lightness Brandley felt in his heart as he prepared for the reception was, he knew, nothing short of a miracle. He was meticulously attired in fawn pantaloons, white silk waistcoat and shirt, and impeccably tied cravat in his favorite mathematical style. Croydon held a long-tailed mulberry coat with gold buttons and slipped it on the baronet's broad shoulders. Croydon then presented Brandley with his high curly beaver hat, gloves, and walking stick.

Brandley set the hat on his black locks at a precise angle, took his gloves, and looked at his walking stick. He took it in his hand. "I don't much need this now. I'm quite recovered from my stupidity." He twirled the stick around in his hand. "But I might purchase an ebony one. It would be convenient should I ever affect to become a dandy." He tossed the stick on his bed with a laugh, realizing the exquisite release from his old feelings. He really didn't mind the stick anymore.

The Cambridge University Press spared no effort for a work they considered monumental. The receiving line included the vice-chancellor of the university as well as chief officers of the Press. The line was interminable. It seemed that every don in the university had accepted the invitation to attend.

Brandley reserved a special handshake for his friend Thomas Deighton, who had been invited at the author's special request. The little bookseller was so thrilled by the affair that he bobbed up and down with his handshake and barely avoided treading on the long academical of the professor ahead of him in the line.

Charlie and Miss Underhill were near the end of the line. "Oh, Sir Brandley, I declare I am quite distracted by the magnitude of your accomplishments." To prove her point Faith dropped her reticule as she held her hand out to him.

Brandley retrieved it for her and presented it with a flourish. "My sisters were quite sunk in the dismals that they couldn't attend to felicitate you too. And Mama —" Here she dropped her fan.

"My turn this time." Charlie bent to pick it up. "Quite sure Hilliard knows you congratulate him." Charlie urged Miss Underhill ahead. "Tell you what, you find a nice seat. I'll bring you a plate from the buffet."

Brandley was aware of one master who had failed to appear — the one he most wished to see. All the hands had been shaken, all congratulations received. Brandley's editor escorted him to the cold collation. With indifference he put a variety of cold meats and jellies on his plate. Then a painful thought wrenched at his heart. *If only Elinor could have shared this moment.*

He turned to find an unoccupied table when the vision appeared before him. The thought of Elinor had been so intense he felt he must have conjured her up. But Dr. Silbert was by her side, and he had done nothing to cause the professor to materialize. Brandley set his plate of food on the table nearest him under the startled nose of the vice-chancellor's fastidious wife and stepped forward.

Elinor seemed to glide toward him in her satin gown. Her head held high, her countenance calm, she was serene.

"Elinor . . ." He held out his hand. She placed hers in it.

"Congratulations, Hilliard," Dr. Silbert said. "Fine piece of work you've produced. It will make your reputation."

"Thank you, sir." Elinor withdrew her hand, and Brandley clasped the professor's.

"My wife was indisposed, so I persuaded my daughter to accompany me." The words were spoken seriously, but Brandley thought he caught a twinkle in the professor's eyes. "Ah, there's Ainsworth. I think I'll just have a word with him if you'll excuse me."

Alone but for the crowd around them, Elinor and Brandley faced each other.

Brandley offered his arm. "Would you care to take some air, Miss Silbert?"

"Thank you, Sir Brandley. I would find that most pleasant." She placed her hand on his bent elbow.

Long evening shadows striped a path made golden by the lowering autumn sun. Fallen leaves crunched under their feet. Along the Backs the willow trees, always the last to lose their leaves, clung with obstinacy to the last thin bits of yellow foliage. They sat down on a bench built round the tree trunk under the drooping boughs.

In all this time not a word had passed between them, and yet the atmosphere was not one of tension, but of a heightened awareness of each other, of great sensitivity.

He turned to her. "Elinor, thank you for allowing me to speak to you. After the abominable, infamous —"

"Wheedle you cut?" Elinor finished for him.

"I thought you would stay with Joan longer. Until you realized you were well out of a bad bargain. Then my bit of gammon wouldn't matter."

"Did it matter to you?" The intensity of the question was increased by the quietness of her voice.

"More than my life." The agony in his

eyes and tenderness in his voice made Elinor catch her breath. "But, Elinor, I've so much to tell you. So much has changed."

"Yes, I can see that."

In glowing terms, Brandley told her of the faith to which Simeon had led him to open his life. "That awful dark void that nothing would fill was suddenly flooded with Light and the assurance of God's power and love — and understanding and acceptance. Elinor, all the old self-hatred simply drained from me. His love took over. Am I making sense?"

Elinor looked steadily into his shining eyes, her heart in her throat. She nodded. She sensed the strength that living with his disability and now rising above it with God's help had given him.

Brandley took her hands. "Now I can love you without reservation, the way Hall said." He paused. "If you'll let me."

She smiled at him with a glow of happiness which gave added bloom to her beauty. "It was worth waiting for. And I do love you most dreadfully."

"And forgive me?"

"And forgive you."

He took her in his arms and kissed her deeply, hungrily. When at last they pulled apart, she rested her head against his chest.

He clasped her to him and gave a little sound between a laugh and a groan. "I came so close to losing you it terrifies me." Then his fierce embrace softened. He held her at arm's length, ravenous to look at her. He saw her joyous, tearful smile and thought he would burst with the happiness within him. Their little world beneath the sheltering, drooping branches of the willow was flooded with the completeness of their joy.

"My very own Daphne. To think I shall see that smile every morning at breakfast for the rest of my life."

"Yes, didn't your classics professor ever tell you? They found a lost manuscript — Daphne and Apollo lived happily ever after."

"A myth with a happy ending? Preposterous!"

The Legend of
Daphne and Apollo

According to Roman mythology, Daphne was an independent young woman who greatly tried her father's patience by rejecting all her handsome and eligible suitors. It took only a smiling hug from his daughter to make her river-god father yield and allow Daphne a degree of freedom unaccustomed to young women of her day.

Apollo happened to come upon her in the woods one day and immediately fell in love with her. When she protested at his advances, he swept her into his arms to carry her from the woods. But Daphne continued to struggle and cried to her father for help. As soon as her request was uttered, thin bark began to replace her glowing skin, her hair was changed to leaves, and her arms became graceful branches.

Daphne was changed into a laurel tree, but Apollo still loved her. In his grief, he cried, "Oh, fairest of maidens, you are lost to me. But you shall forever be my tree. With your leaves my victors shall wreathe their brows. Apollo and his laurel shall be joined together wherever songs are sung and stories told."

TIME LINE

The Cambridge Chronicles

United States		England
George Whitefield begins preaching	1738	John Wesley's Aldersgate experience
French and Indian War	1756	
	1760	George III crowned
	1760	Lady Huntingdon opens chapel in Bath
	1766	Stamp Act passed
Boston Tea Party	1773	Rowland Hill ordained
The Revolutionary War	1776	The American War
	1787	Wilberforce begins antislavery campaign
Constitution ratified	1788	
George Washington elected President	1789	
	1799	Church Missionary Society founded

	1805	Lord Nelson wins Battle of Trafalgar
	1807	Parliament bans slave trade
War of 1812	1812	Charles Simeon begins Conversation Parties
	1815	Waterloo
Missouri Compromise	1820	George IV crowned
John Quincy Adams elected President	1825	
	1830	William IV crowned
Temperance Union founded	1833	William Wilberforce dies
Texas Independence	1836	Charles Simeon dies
	1837	Queen Victoria crowned
Susan B. Anthony Campaigns	1848	
California Gold Rush	1849	
	1851	Crystal palace opens
Uncle Tom's Cabin published	1852	
	1854	Florence Nightingale goes to Crimean War

Abraham Lincoln elected President	**1860**	
Emancipation Proclamation	**1863**	
	1865	Hudson Taylor founds China Inland Mission
Transcontinental Railroad completed	**1869**	
	1877	D. L. Moody and Ira Sankey London revivals
Thomas Edison invents light bulb	**1879**	
	1885	Cambridge Seven join China Inland Mission

Word List

Academical — academic costume worn by member of university

Alfresco — outdoors

Bamming — to impose on one a falsity, hoaxing

Bedell — university officer who walks at the head of processions of officers and students (bedell at Cambridge; bedel at Oxford)

Bellerphon — mortal who rode Pegasus, was thrown off, and crippled for deigning to ride to the gods

Bluestocking — woman who was, or pretended to be, intellectual

Blunt — ready cash, money

Bum squabble — mislead, hoodwink, bamboozle

Capability Brown — a famous English landscape architect

Cawker — youngster, immature

Change ringing — English bell ringing in which the bells change in varying patterns

Chiaroscuro — pictorial treatment of light and dark, sharp contrast

Curricle — two-wheeled carriage drawn by two horses

Coze — chat

Danae — beautiful maiden Zeus appeared to as a shower of gold and then seduced

Epergne — branched gold or silver centerpiece

Europa — beautiful maiden Zeus appeared to as a white bull and then seduced

Fustian — pretentious nonsense

Gammon — talk intended to deceive; humbug

Gig — one-horse carriage

Hall — meals served in the common dining room of an English college

Hartshorn — powdered antlers, used as gelatin

Inwit — conscience, understanding

Leda — Queen of Sparta who, after being seduced by Zeus in the form of a swan, gave birth to Helen

Levee — formal reception

Maggot — sudden, silly idea, whim

Motte — hill serving as a site for a Norman castle

Ninnyhammer — fool, simpleton, ninny

Nitter-natter — chitchat

Noddicock — simpleton, fool

Nuncheon — light, uncooked snack taken in the middle of the day

On dit — gossip

On tenterhooks — in a state of uneasiness, strain, suspense

Pelisse — woman's loose, light-weight cloak

Point non plus — dueling term meaning stalemate (point not either)

Puce — dark red

Quiz — mock, tease

Quizzing glass — monocle

Mrs. Radcliffe — popular Gothic novelist of the day

Rout — fashionable gathering, reception

Sapskull — senseless, foolish fellow

Shabster — one who engages in shabby conduct

Sporting the fives — engage in a boxing match

Starched-up — stiff, prim, formal, affected

Syllabub — a frothy, sweet dessert made of cream and liquor

Take her in shift — take her without a dowry

Thomas Rowlandson — famous English caricaturist

Ton — smart set, fashionable, London social leaders

Vinaigrette — smelling salts

Weston — best-known tailor of the day

Wheedle — to decoy by insinuation, run a scam

Bibliography

Brown, Abner William. *Recollections of the Conversation Parties of the Reverend Charles Simeon, M.A.* London: Hamilton Adams, 1863.

Brown, Ford K. *Fathers of the Victorians.* Cambridge: Cambridge University Press, 1961.

Cooper, C. H. *Annals of Cambridge, 1688–1849.* 4 Vols.

Hopkins, Hugh Evan. *Charles Simeon of Cambridge.* Grand Rapids: Eerdmans, 1977.

_____. *Charles Simeon, Preacher Extraordinary.* Brancote Notts: Grove Books, 1979.

MacDonald, George. *Creation in Christ.* Ed. Rolland Hein. From *Unspoken Sermons*, 3 Vols. Wheaton: Harold Shaw Publishers, 1976.

Meade, William. *A Faithful Servant, The Life and Labors of the Reverend Charles Simeon,* selected from the larger work of the Reverend William Carus. New York: Depository of Protestant Episcopal Society for Promotion of Evangelical Knowledge, 1853.

Scholar of the period (i.e., by William Hill

Tucker, 1803–1901). *King's Old Court 1822–1825.* Typed transcript. Used by permission of Kings College.

Teichiman, Oskar. *The Cambridge Undergraduate 100 Years Ago.* W. Heffes, 1926.

Winstanley, D. A. *Early Victorian Cambridge.* Cambridge: Cambridge University Press, 1955.

_____. *Unreformed Cambridge.* Cambridge: Cambridge University Press, 1935.

The Works of the Reverend Robert Hall. First complete edition, with a brief memoir of the author, 2 Vols. New York: G. & C. & H. Carvill, 1930.